I AM THE WIND

By

Rayford E. Hammond

5-22-09

TO TERRI —

MAY ALL YOU TEARS BE TEARS

OF JOY.

ALWAYS,

Ray H.

PENMAN PUBLISHING, INC.

Copyright © 2000 Rayford E. Hammond

Penman Publishing, Inc.
4159 Ringgold Road, Suite 104
Chattanooga, Tennessee 37412

All rights reserved. Use of any part of this publication without prior written consent of the publisher is an infringement of the copyright law.

Rayford E. Hammond
I AM THE WIND

Dedication

- To my own Lara, whose real name was Pamela Dawn. Like Lara in the narrative, Pamela was born November 10, 1972 and died in an automobile accident on January 24, 1990, while en route to school. Although this is a work of fiction, I have attempted to embody in Lara, from whose viewpoint this story is told, many of the characteristics associated with the life and death of my daughter.

- To my living daughters, Tania and Tammy, whose composite character in this narrative is Lara's sister, Tracy.

- To my grandchildren, Shannon, Kacie and Cody, who are most significant in helping me in my struggle to live with this loss.

- To my wife, Mary Lee, who has no direct counterpart in this chronicle, primarily because our feelings are so intertwined that she is better depicted herein as being one with Lara's father.

- To all who may have suffered this most devastating of tragedies: the loss of a child.

Memorial Tribute

Do not stand at my grave and weep,
I am not there; I do not sleep.
I am a thousand winds that blow,
I am the diamond's gilt on snow.
I am the sunlight on ripened grain,
I am the gentle autumn's rain.
When you awaken in the morning's hush,
I am the swift uplifting rush
Of quiet birds in circled flight,
I am the soft stars that shine at night.
Do not stand at my grave and cry,
I am not there; I did *not* die.

- Author unknown

Note From the Author

When I first began this work, it was never my intention to publish it as a book; moreover, I never even intended for anyone else to read this feeble attempt to relate in words those innermost feelings of my heart—a task that is of course impossible to accomplish.

As time passed, I began to accept and understand that this most awful of tragedies is not unique to me and my family; that indeed, countless others have had to endure equally—if not moreso—devastating misfortunes. Over a period of years, I gradually concluded that perhaps this fictionalized account of how one father went about attempting to cope with his terrible loss could perhaps be of help to others in similar circumstances.

If there is one thing that I have learned throughout this ordeal, it is that someone who has never experienced the loss of a child could ever possibly comprehend the effect this has on a person. We all say, of course, that we understand; but how could one ever imagine putting themselves in this type situation and experiencing the indescribable feelings that occur deep within? In truth, no one ever could.

Every parent of a teenager has probably tried to imagine what it might be like to receive that *dreaded* phone call some night when their teenager is late returning home. We all imagine the worst sometimes, and when the phone rings and our child is not yet home, we often cringe, fearing to answer the call, convinced that something awful has happened. Of course, we do not really believe this; and if the phone call were to come advising us that our son or daughter had been killed in an automobile accident, we would not be able to believe it, even then. There would have to have been some mistake, we tell ourselves, for our psyche is not equipped to accept that this most horrible thing could actually happen to us.

But when it does happen to us, we of course find that we have no choice but to search for some way to go on; and as time passes, we are forced to begin to seek some way of coping with what we have already concluded is something we will never be able to overcome. For when a child dies in the prime of their life, a part of the parent dies with them. We may know logically that we must find a way to go on; but inside, we gradually accept that nothing will ever again seem quite right.

So, each person, in their own way, must come to an understanding of how they will go on living.

Unfortunately, some never reach this state. That does not mean that they decide to take their own life; but the effect is frequently almost the same—they choose to continue to *exist*, but never again can they allow themselves to *live* life to its fullest.

Although this account of one father's struggle to find a way to live with his terrible loss is obviously fictional—after all, the story is told from the point of view of the departed child, commencing on the day she is killed—the feelings expressed herein are as real as this author could possibly convey in mere words. This is written *from the heart,* with no attempt to conceal any of those most awful deep feelings of anger, and at times loss of faith in a higher being, that most likely occur to every person going through this sort of tragedy, which seems so unnatural, for we think we are supposed to die before our children die. And we ask ourselves how, if there is a God, could he possibly allow this to happen. Then we sometimes decide that it must have been designed as a punishment for us, that we should have—could have—been a better parent; that we should have been able to prevent this from happening to *our* child.

Are there answers to these countless questions everyone asks in their effort to deal with something like this? Some find solace in their religion; others take different routes; some become alcoholics;

some become worse! Will this book help others who are going through similar circumstances? It is my fervent belief and hope that it will; that from reading this account, others may at least come to understand that they are not alone; that perhaps it is even all right to ask those most awful questions; even to conclude that there cannot possibly be a God. For we must each find a way that works for us in dealing with this sort of tragedy.

It is hoped that perhaps just by learning that we are not alone, that someone else has also screamed at God in the night, and has asked those countless unanswerable questions, mostly beginning with the word "why"; that someone else also nearly drives themself crazy playing the "what if" game, that this will help in some small way. And if this be true, then therein lies my reason for deciding to publish this book.

Should anyone reading this account feel that it might help someone they know, perhaps someone who has also lost a child, then please refer them to me and I will see that they get a copy.

> In Love and Tears,
> Rayford E. Hammond

Chapter One

I am here! I do not yet know why I am *here*, or exactly how I came to be *here*, or even where *here* might be. Not only do I comprehend that I am *here*, I also somehow know that I always have been and always will be, although how I came to know these things remains a mystery. Yet, this hardly matters, for I am still *Lara*, and I am *here*!

As I look around, things appear nearly the same as before, yet somehow different. For example, I seem to be able to move faster and easier now, almost as if I can float from place to place. Strange as it seems, I may even be able to *think* myself from one place to another.

Probably I should not have used the term *look around*. I suppose I only *thought* around, since in the physical sense I can no longer see. Now that I think about it, I doubt that I can hear, smell or taste either. Could I be only imagining these sounds, odors and flavors that remain a part of my being? Although nearly certain that I can still feel, possibly that, too, might only be imagined. Naturally, I cannot feel physically because that old body no longer works. Of this I am certain, for I saw it in its mangled, useless state: *dead* they called it. Perhaps I should say I *discerned* it in that state, rather than *saw* it, but since it still feels like seeing, I will continue to use that term to describe the sensation.

The last thing I remember seeing before being *here* was my body lying on a bed or a table in a hospital emergency room. Suddenly I am becoming aware that I am *not* in that body. Strangely, I feel as if I am above looking down, watching and listening as two young doctors try to find a pulse, a breath, any sign of life in my body. *Almost like in the movies*, I think as I try to accept the reality of this new form, which feels nearly as I always imagined it would, only amazingly better as I seem to float above everything. Of course, I cannot be certain that I am actually up here. Perhaps I am merely imagining this strange sensation, which feels similar to watching myself in a dream. Yet this feels much stronger and somehow more real.

Suddenly, I hear someone speaking. "We've lost her! She's gone."

I AM NOT GONE! *I'm here*! Why are these people unable to hear me? I feel as if I am speaking, although possibly the words exist only in my mind.

Wherever I am now, I do not want to go back. Everything here is so peaceful and I feel remarkably free. I thought dying was supposed to be painful, but I cannot remember feeling any pain. I am not certain, of course, that I *am* dead. Out of my body? *Yes*, or so it seems. What else could that mean? And besides, the doctor just pronounced me *dead*. Yet how can this be, if I am still *here*? Although I do not understand this state in which I find myself, I somehow sense that it is right; exactly as things are meant to be.

I begin to recall the events leading up to my being *here.* I remember waking up this morning and thinking, *Oh no! Look at the time! I'm gonna be late for school again. Guess Lynn and I stayed out too late last night. Gotta hurry!*

Scrambling out of bed, I quickly dress and brush my teeth. On my way through the kitchen, I grab a banana. In the garage, I jump into Dad's old 1985 Honda Accord that he has been allowing me drive for the past few months. As I back hurriedly out of the driveway, I notice the morning is cool, but bright and sunny. I take a moment to observe how beautiful the lake appears as I drive along the road that meanders around the deep blue water, which appears so still, with hardly a ripple. I notice a lone man in a small boat casting with his fly rod against the far shore. Does he think spring is here already—in January?

Spring? At the end of this springtime, I will be graduating from high school. How weird. And I have no idea what I will do then. College? Dad seems to think so, as do many of my friends, but I am still not sure. Unless my grades improve, I may not have a choice, of course, so I suppose I had better buckle down from here on, or I might not even graduate on time.

Upon reaching the main highway, I turn onto the narrow, two-lane road that snakes its way through six miles of beautiful rolling farmland. By now I have this whole stretch of road memorized, having made the trip frequently during the past three years, often as many as three or four times a day. Although I have only been driving for a few months, already I feel as if I could navigate this road with my eyes closed. The little Honda seems to know the way, needing only an occasional urge of encouragement when entering some of the sharper turns.

While lighting my first cigarette, I quickly increase speed to seventy-five miles per hour. Dad has warned me that using the cruise control on this winding road is unsafe, but I decide to set the cruise anyway. After all, I still have to put on my lipstick and fix my hair. Besides, as I said, I could navigate this road in my sleep, and there is hardly any traffic at this time of the morning.

As I top the hill approaching that sharp

curve near the old house that advertises antiques, I adjust the rear-view mirror so that I can see myself. Confirming that my hair is a mess, I fling my cigarette out the window and reach into my bag for a hairbrush. When I locate the brush, I begin pulling out some of the tangles. The car careens around the next curve as I glance back and forth between the road and my image in the rear-view mirror. Suddenly, I notice the dashboard clock. *Oh my God! Only five minutes till first bell*! I punch the cruise on up to eighty and begin searching for my lipstick.

Suddenly, from the corner of my eye I glimpse the road ahead: *Oh, God! I'm on the WRONG side of the road!* Thank goodness there are no cars coming from the other direction. But since I cannot see over the hill directly ahead, I quickly swerve back to the right, causing the Honda's tires to scream as they skid on the pavement. Fighting now to stay in the road, I realize I might be going a little fast, so I tap the brake pedal to disengage the cruise control.

The warning, *Never hit the brakes when in*

a skid, either from drivers' education or from Dad, flashes into my mind as I fight the steering wheel.

The front wheels suddenly slide off the pavement onto the graveled shoulder and I try to remember what to do in a front-wheel-drive car to recover from a skid. I have to do something fast, so I jerk the wheel back to the left and the skid reverses. Panic overcomes me as the car continues to fishtail down the road, sometimes on the pavement, sometimes off.

As I feel the rear wheels sliding farther into the ditch, I fight the wheel harder. Suddenly the car leaves the road completely and I feel a terrible jolt as the Honda slams into something alongside the road.

Suddenly the car slams onto its side and begins rolling . . . over and over . . . bouncing . . . crashing down on its top . . . sailing through the air . . . bouncing again. Horrible metallic crashing sounds! Glass breaking! Someone screaming!

In my panic, I try to remember if my seatbelt was fastened. Although nearly certain that it was, I am still being thrown about in all directions. Then the car smashes into something solid and it envelops me like a vice. *Oh, God, I'm being crushed.*

Then all motion ceases.

Next, I sense the sounds of flowing liquid, hissing steam and gurgling liquid. An acrid stench of gasoline fills my nostrils. Somewhere a radio is playing and I imagine I am hearing my favorite song, *After All*, from that movie called *Chances Are.* Did I have the radio on before the crash? Probably so, since I seldom turned it off.

I try to move but find that something is restraining me. I feel as if I am trapped underwater and I gasp for breath as a warm substance bathes my face, covering me until I am drifting in the substance, floating into it, becoming a part of it.

Then there is only blackness.

Sometime later, I dream that I hear a faint sound of sirens in the distance. Now a man is speaking. "My God! Her chest is crushed . . . head too . . . gonna be tough gettin' her outta here."

Then another voice: "Worst I've ever seen, Bill. Don't see no way she's gonna make it."

What does he mean, *don't see no way she's gonna make it*?

Everything remains dreamlike as apparently I float in and out of consciousness. First I am cold, and then hot. I try to speak, to call for Dad, but I still have hardly any breath.

Next, I imagine I am in an ambulance, and I hear more sirens. Someone then places something over my face, and I cannot see or move. I hear a man talking about me as if I am not here. He is saying horrible things about my body.

"Chest crushed, fractured skull, BP eighty over forty, pulse too weak to measure. We're administering oxygen . . . I think we're losing her . . . roger, we're about five minutes away."

The next thing I remember is watching those events taking place in that hospital emergency room. And then it is over as someone pulls a sheet over the face of the young girl they called *Lara*.

I AM HERE! I scream as loudly as I can. *Lara is NOT GONE*, I shout from somewhere above. But no one seems to hear; obviously, the words are only in my mind.

I watch now as they wheel the body that I so recently occupied out of the emergency room and down a corridor. Where are they taking my body? *Oh, God! Not the morgue!*

In the distance, I hear a woman's voice. "Have her parents been notified?"

Then I remember that Dad is not here. He is out of town, and I try to tell them that I know where he is. He is visiting my sister, Tracy, who lives in Knoxville, the nearest large city, about seventy miles away. Dad went to help her move into her new apartment. He tried to get me to go with him, but of course, I refused, using the excuse that I did not want to miss school today, but the real reason was that I wanted to go to Steve's party tonight. But I guess I will miss that party, after all.

Whoa! What is happening? All at once, I find myself there with Dad and Tracy. They are just finishing breakfast and are laughing and talking; obviously, they do not yet know.

Now how can this be? I am in the hospital, yet I'm not; I'm here with Dad and Tracy. How did I get here so fast?

Suddenly a telephone rings and Tracy answers.

"Hello . . . yes . . . yes . . . Nooooooo . . ."

She falls to the floor and covers her face with her hands. Dad grabs the phone, and after a few words are exchanged, he slumps to the floor beside Tracy. He drops the phone and his whole body jerks as he sobs. Somehow, I know the caller was Dad's friend, Andy Parrish, calling to give Dad and Tracy the horrible news. Poor Andy, I wonder how he got Tracy's new phone number; but of course, that is of no matter now.

As Dad and Tracy hold each other and sob, I try to tell them, to *think* to them: *Dad, Tracy, I'm okay; I'm here.* But they do not hear.

I am surprised that I can share Dad's feelings as his heart breaks. Then I realize that I am aware of everything he is feeling, and Tracy, too. *It's all right,* I continue to try to tell them. *I'm here! I'm okay!*

But they do not listen. I scream the

thoughts, yet they do not hear.

As Dad and Tracy begin the dreadful drive back to our house, I find myself in the car with them. Dad is in a semi-trance, but he insists on driving. I continue to feel his every emotion. Primarily, he is experiencing disbelief, his mind unable accept that this awful thing has happened.

I think now of a movie I saw recently about a similar situation, where a man died but was not really *gone* in that he could still see, hear and feel, just as before; yet, no one else seemed to be aware that he was among them. Sometimes they sensed that *something* was there, some presence, although not the person—merely an illusion, they thought. Just the mind playing tricks.

The mind! Suddenly I wonder if I still have a mind. Surely I must, for I can reason and feel; and I am still *Lara*, in the sense that I know the things I knew before, and perhaps more. Maybe a mind is all I am now. Or a soul? Could I be just a soul now? I know, of course, that I am no longer in my physical body, yet I feel as if I am, since I seem to be able to move about.

I remain with Dad and Tracy throughout the trip, trying to comfort them. Surely, they must feel my presence. Finally, we are home. As we enter our house, I notice that things look the same as I remember from this morning. In the garage, I see my little Honda motor scooter that Dad bought me for my fourteenth birthday three years ago when we first moved here. I feel Dad's dread at ever having to look at that bike again. He feels his heart will break again every time he sees it.

Once more, I try to tell him, *It's okay, Dad. I am fine*. But it is no use. Why are they not aware that I am with them?

Later, I watch as Tracy sorts through the several items that I left scattered about my bedroom. Dad has asked her if she will arrange my things. *What a mess*, I think, feeling embarrassment at having left my room in such a state. I *think* a gasp as my sister finds a note that I recently wrote to my best friend, Lynn. *Please don't read it*, I *think* to her, and she does not, although probably not because I *thought* her not to do it. Instead, she places the note inside a box where I have kept everything I have ever written through the years: my journals, diaries, and notes to and from friends. I shudder, wondering if Tracy or Dad will ever read these things. It would be so embarrassing if they ever did. But for some reason, I do not think they will. Then I remember that note I wrote to Dad just a few days ago; the one I never gave him. I do wish he could read that.

Tracy spends a long time in my room, and I feel her anguish as she organizes my things, looking at each item for a few moments, holding it, feeling a connection, and then experiencing an awful emptiness. Tears fill her eyes and I want to comfort her, yet I cannot. Soon my room looks better than it has looked in months and Tracy leaves the room, closing the door behind her.

Wait! I yell, but she is gone. Then suddenly I am in the living room with her and Dad. Did I just float through that closed door?

A few of Dad's friends have come to visit tonight, including his best friend, Andy

Parrish. Andy and Dad are the same age and have been friends since soon after we moved here. They play golf and tennis together, and Dad helps Andy with some computer work at Andy's place of business. Andy lost his wife a few years ago and has never remarried either, so he and Dad have that in common.

Andy stays with Dad and Tracy long after the others have gone. They try to comfort Dad, but nothing seems to help. I hear them discussing the memorial service scheduled for tomorrow evening. Dad cannot even imagine how he will ever get through this event. And then there is the funeral scheduled for the following morning. He wonders how he will ever survive these services.

Finally, Andy leaves, and soon Tracy talks Dad into going to bed. But he does not sleep, and long before daylight he is up, walking through the now quiet, empty-feeling house. After a while he slumps into a chair in the family room and just sits there, his head in his hands. I think he still cannot believe that the accident actually happened and that I am gone.

Dad is still sitting in the chair later when

Tracy gets up to fix breakfast. Since sunrise, he has been sitting in this chair, staring out the window toward the lake. With intense dread, he thinks of the long day ahead and the memorial service this evening, and again wonders how he will ever muster the strength to get through it. I feel his silent prayer, asking God to help him to endure.

I'll be here to help, Dad, I think as strongly as I can, but he still does not seem to be aware of my presence. Although I do not know how, I have to find some way to let him know that I love him and that I am all right.

Chapter Two

*T*onight I watch as more than two hundred of my friends and family members, including nearly everyone from my high school senior class, file into the small funeral parlor. They canceled school today, just because of my memorial service tonight. I also see several of Dad's friends here, and strangely, I can sense what these people are thinking and feeling. Some mourn my passing, others appear confused, and a few seem to experience no feelings at all. I try to *think* to everyone the right words they might say to Dad to help him get through this ordeal, but I cannot determine how successful I am at this.

My most difficult moment occurs a few minutes later when my best friend, Lynn, comes forward to look at me—the old me. Unable to control her emotions, she breaks down as she approaches the coffin.

"NO, NO . . . You *CAN'T* be gone! Noooo!" Lynn covers her face with her hands and sobs uncontrollably.

I stare at the body with Lynn, sharing her pain and trying to comfort her. I notice that they have made the body look good, completely covering the place where my head was crushed. And I actually like the way they fixed my long, dark hair, framing it around my face, creating wisps above my forehead held in place with hair spray, almost exactly as I usually fixed it. I remember how Dad often kidded me about how long it took me to fix my hair every morning before school. Dad and Tracy had them dress me—the body—in my favorite pair of old jeans, the ones with holes in the knees, and a new pink sweater that Dad gave me for Christmas, only a few weeks ago. Sadly, I had never even worn the sweater. I notice that I am still wearing my watch and rings, along with my favorite earrings, which Tracy must have picked out, because I do not remember putting them on. Of course, the body can only be seen from the chest up, but I can sense everything else.

It's okay, Lynnie. I'm here. No, not there— here. Look around. I'm all around you. Can't you feel me?

I try to touch her, to hug her, but she ignores me, as if I am not even here. Of course, she thinks I am gone. I sense her feeling guilty now about an argument we had recently over some silly something, probably a boy. I cannot even remember now; but of course, that does not matter anymore. *It's okay, Lynnie*, I think as loudly as I dare. Can one think loudly, I wonder? I sense Lynn's every emotion, and as she sobs, I try to make my heart become one with hers. Just for an instant, she seems to feel me here with her, but then Lynn's mother comes and leads her away.

NO! Don't go, Lynnie! Don't leave me!

But of course, she cannot leave me, for I am not *there;* I am *here*.

A few minutes later, Lynn goes outside into the foyer, and I remain with her as she tries to talk with some of our friends who are gathered there. Many are crying as they hug each other, uncertain what to say or do. Of course, they do not understand; nor do I. Yet, I think I understand more than they do. I do not know why the accident occurred, or what has actually happened to me, but I know the most important thing of all: I am *here*. I am not gone—or *dead*, as they call it. *Lara still exists.* Why do they not know this?

My next and most difficult moment occurs when Dad approaches to view the body. Tracy and Andy walk with him, one on either side, holding his arms. They stop before the coffin and stare silently down at the remains of their Lara. Dad does not cry, but I can feel his anguish and his broken heart. I understand why he did not at first want to view my body, but now I feel him becoming glad that he did. Yet, this is the hardest thing he has ever had to do because he wants to remember me as before, when I was alive. As with Lynn, I think: *It's okay; I'm here.* But of course, Dad does not hear me either.

The funeral service is to be tomorrow, so I stay with Dad tonight, as does my sister, Tracy. Dad does not know how he will ever survive the ordeal. I was glad to learn that the funeral is not to be strictly a religious service. It will be conducted by a minister, though—Reverend Evans, whom I knew, although I seldom attended church. I wonder if that is going to matter now.

Everyone again gathers at the funeral home this morning, this place I remember passing so often on my way to and from school. Never once did I consider its purpose, as death was not something with which I needed to be concerned. I already know that the music to be played today is music that either Dad or I liked, and not those grim songs often heard at funerals. And I am pleased with Dad's choice. I would have died again had they played *Shall We Gather at the River* or *The Old Rugged Cross*. Why people choose to create the type images these kinds of songs depict has always puzzled me.

At first, I think it strange as the service begins with the playing of a Johnny Mathis song entitled *Chances Are*. When the first few notes of this song sound through the speakers mounted on either side of the parlor, I hear and feel my friends begin to weep, some silently and some loudly. And I become sad with them. Then suddenly I remember; of course, how could I have forgotten? One of the last happy events that Dad and I shared during my last few weeks *there* was that movie called *Chances Are*. It was about a young man, played by Robert Downey, Jr., and I remember he was killed, then later came back as another person and tried to resume his relationship with his previous wife, played by Cybil Shepherd. Now I understand that this is Dad's way of saying *I love you and miss you*.

As Reverend Evans begins speaking, I find it weird hearing him talking about me as if I am not here. But then I remind myself that they do not know I *am*. The minister speaks primarily to my friends, trying to help them understand why these kinds of things happen. I do not know if what he says is correct, but his words seem to help my friends feel some better. I understand that the funeral is not for me; it is for those left behind, and that is how I would have had it be.

When Reverend Evans finishes his remarks, I am again confused as another song, *Smoke Gets In Your Eyes*, begins playing through the speakers. I cannot imagine why they are playing this song, which also seems to make everyone cry, as if smoke is getting in their eyes.

Sometime later, I watch from the tops of some tall maple trees growing behind the cemetery as the small procession turns into this remote country burial ground nearly a hundred miles from where we lived. The sky is gray and overcast and a slight breeze causes the treetops to sway gently as the long, black hearse pulls up alongside a green tent with a few chairs sitting underneath. Some men then remove the coffin and place Lara, or what they think of as Lara, over the hole that is to be her final resting-place. The grave is next to my mother's, whose body has been here for several years already. I vaguely remember having been here before, the day my mother was buried, but I was only five years old then and cannot remember much. I do remember looking up at these same treetops, though, and wondering if my mother might be up there in the breeze, watching as I am now. It makes me happy to know that she must have been. I wonder where she is now, and if I might see her soon.

Only a few close friends and family members have made the long trip across the state to this burial place. I listen now as a different minister attempts to comfort them. He also believes that he is saying the right things, but his words do not seem to help much. After a while, I float down to where Dad is standing. I can feel him already beginning to blame himself and I try to tell him: *It was NOT your fault, Dad. There was nothing you could have done to prevent the accident.* He feels guilty that he was not at home that morning, but of course, that would have made no difference; I would have driven to school anyway, as I usually did. Andy and Tracy have already told Dad these things, but he still feels responsible.

Oh Dad, please don't blame yourself. It was MY fault, not yours, I shout, but he does not hear. Why can I not reach him?

It bothers me that these people do not know I am *here* with them. In my mind, I scream: *LOOK AT ME, all you people. I'm here! I'm in the trees. Can you not see the leaves blowing in the wind?*

Just then, Dad looks up toward the treetops and immediately I feel that he *knows.* I am overjoyed. *Dad KNOWS I am here! He KNOWS*! I can feel him understanding that I am in the wind blowing through the treetops, that perhaps *I am the wind*, and that I will be all right after all. He may later rationalize that his mind was simply playing tricks, and he might forget that he felt my presence here today. But for this instant, he *knows*; and I am happy.

Along with my family and friends, I watch as Lara's body is lowered slowly into the ground. Lynnie comes and places a rose atop the box that she thinks contains her friend, and then I feel her begin to understand that *Lara* is not in that box. She does not know where I am, although she seems to comprehend that the body in that box is no longer *Lara*. I rejoice when I realize Lynn knows that *I still am*—somewhere, somehow.

Next, I stand with Dad and Tracy as they pause, heads bowed, above my grave, saying their final good-byes.

Then finally it is over, and the people begin departing the small cemetery. Dad remains at a distance for a few minutes, standing underneath the tall maples, not wanting to leave me here alone. I *think* to him: *I'll be all right, Dad. I'm not going to stay here.* I do remain for a while, though, watching as some men fill the hole with dirt. This makes me sad, although I do not know why, for Lara is not in that hole. Then they create a small mound on top and pile it high with all the flowers—so many! More than I ever had while I was living, which seems strange.

Finally, I decide to leave, but suddenly I realize I do not know where I am going. Yet, I cannot stay here. My loved ones may return to this place to visit me from time to time, but I will not be here. They may think they feel my presence, though; and who knows, perhaps I *will* be able to meet them here.

I watch as the last few cars drive slowly

away. There are no more tears now as I visit inside each car, observing the reactions of my loved ones as they leave their concept of my final resting-place. As I listen to the conversation taking place inside Dad's car, I realize the members of my immediate family are en route to a movie theater. *A movie*! I am shocked that they would choose this particular time to go to see a movie. Dad calls the movie *Always,* and explains to the other family members that he and Tracy saw this movie the night before my accident and had thought that I would love the movie. He told them that he had planned to take me to see it when he returned home the next day.

As I watch the movie, *Always,* with them now, I begin to understand. When the song, *Smoke Gets In Your Eyes*, starts to play, things begin to become clear to me. This movie is about a man called Pete, played by Richard Dreyfus, my all-time favorite actor. Pete is killed in a plane crash and is then sent back to help those he left behind; to free his loved ones, primarily his girlfriend, Dorinda, played by

Holly Hunter, and his best friend, Al, played by John Goodman. Pete's spiritual assignment, given to him by an angel played by Audrey Hepburn, is to release those he left behind so they can go on with their lives. Pete can see and hear Al and Dorinda, but they are at first unaware of his presence. Occasionally, they do feel or sense things that he is thinking, and in the end, they become aware of his presence and understand that it is all right to let him go so they can get on with their lives.

As we walk out of the theater, I think: *You did take me to the movie, Dad. And I loved it. And I do understand.*

As I continue to think about that movie and the songs, I begin to figure out more. The song, *Chances Are,* representing one of the last good times Dad and I shared, tells of the beginning of a love affair, perhaps my beginning. Could that be why Dad chose to have them play that song at the beginning of the service? The song, *Smoke Gets In Your Eyes*, representing Dad's last memory of me when I was alive, describes the ending of a love affair, perhaps my ending. He had them play this song as the service ended, perhaps as a way of saying goodbye to his Lara, whom he must love with all his heart.

Some other members of my family, especially my grandparents, do not yet understand and silently question why Dad chose to play such non-traditional songs at a funeral. They also think he is crazy for attending a movie right after his daughter has just been buried. This does not matter, of course, because I understand perfectly, as does Tracy. I hope someday everyone else will understand, but all that matters now is that Dad and I know.

Smoke gets in my eyes—or perhaps I should say I experience the crying feeling—whenever I hear the song, which is frequently because Dad plays it often. Smoke gets in his eyes, too, when he listens, but he and I both understand that this is good for him. Tears wash away the grief, they say. Dad has not yet found that tape in my stereo containing the other song from the movie, *Chances Are.* This song, called *After All*, was recorded by Cher and Peter Cetera. I bought the tape the day after we saw the movie, and I played that song repeatedly. Perhaps sometime soon I will find a way to let Dad know that the tape is still there in my tape player.

Chapter Three

We have been home for a few days now, as time is measured *there*. *Home?* Can I still call this home? All the people have gone now, leaving Dad alone—or so he thinks. Tracy tried to persuade him to spend a night or two with her, but Dad told her that he needed to be alone, so finally she returned home.

As Dad walks through the lonely rooms now, I feel his every memory, his pain, his loss and his guilt, for he continues to blame himself for the accident. He doesn't go into my room, and I understand why he feels as if he can never again open that door. Once more, I try to tell him: *Everything's fine. I'm all right. I'm still here. It was NOT your fault.* But it is no use. Occasionally, I can feel a glimmer of understanding in his heart, and for an instant, he feels that I might still exist. I understand that he cannot yet fully accept the reality that this thing happened, that I am gone. Mostly he imagines that I can only live in his heart and mind now.

Before long, I begin to become more curious about where I am. I must be someplace different; yet, it does not seem so. I remember having read and heard stories of people who have gone through near-death experiences and returned to tell about it. I have not yet seen those things so often mentioned in those accounts, such as a tunnel or a bright white light, but the feelings described in those stories, the intense love and peace, have much in common with how I am now feeling. Everything I can see, however, is still *there*, as I call the place where I lived before, and I do not feel that I am in a different place at all.

Perhaps this might be all there is. Maybe I *am* still *there*, simply in a different state of being. I find it strange that I can see and hear everyone *there*, yet they cannot see or hear me, and I wonder if things will continue this way. Of course, when I think about it, I understand *why* they cannot see or hear me; no longer am

I in my physical body. I still feel like *Lara*, though, and I want them to know that I *am*. Yet, I fear they may never understand.

Many of Dad's questions are similar to my own, and we each realize that some of the things we are thinking now would appear crazy to most people. Dad is trying to define where I might be and why this had to happen. I understand what he is trying to do. He needs to make some sense of it all, to find a reason why his Lara was killed. Neither he nor I know the reason, though, and perhaps we never will.

I cringe as Dad begins to play the *Why* game, followed by the *What-if* game. *Why* did this have to happen? *Why* did I let her have a car? *What-if* I had been at home? *What-if* we had never moved to this place? *Why* Lara? *Why* me? He knows this is not what he should be doing; yet, he cannot seem to stop.

Soon Dad begins to realize that nearly everything he once felt was so important hardly matters at all anymore. And small things that meant nothing before begin to assume a much greater significance. He feels that everything is out of balance, and is uncertain what he believes anymore, especially about things like God and life after death. Somehow, I sense that everything is in perfect harmony, although I do not know why this happened, or why I feel this way. I believe everything is as it should be, though; everything except Dad, who keeps asking himself what purpose there is for him to go on living. I want to answer this question, to scream it to him, and I try; but of course, he does not hear me.

I begin to wonder if Dad is going crazy; or am I? I can sense his every question, almost as if we are talking. It occurs to me that although I may learn the answers to some of his questions, I might never be able to tell him, and this makes me sad.

Today Dad is wondering about the concept of *now*, whether now is a time, a place or simply a condition. If *now* is a time, is it the beginning of the remainder of time, he wonders? Or is it the ending of a previous time? He knows it is both, but I feel him decide to view his *now* as a dot on a time line representing the end of a previous time. I fear this is a mistake, for by so viewing it, he may feel that life is depressing, worthless and hopeless. Yet if he views *now* as the beginning of the remainder of time, then I suppose that might frighten him even more, and he would only continue to worry about his unknown future.

I begin to feel as if this may be all there is or ever was or ever will be. Perhaps *now* is a combination of all past, present and future events. And possibly *now* bears no relation at all to *time*. Could it be that everything is somehow happening all at the same time? Assuming time even exists. It seems that time is of less importance wherever I am now, although I do not yet understand how this can be. I realize, of course, that time is used primarily for measuring the movement of physical things, and I suppose, therefore, that since there are no physical things *here*, there might be no need for time. This is all way too deep for me to understand, although I do seem to comprehend a little more than I did at first.

I still do not know where I am. From all I now know, and from what I am able to sense, I am still *there*. I realize, however, that I am no longer physically in that dimension. But I feel as if I am in a physical place, and that I am in a body—not physical, of course, but still a body. I see all the things I saw before, yet I am no longer physically a part of those things.

I begin to wonder, since I can see what Dad sees, will I be able in some way to affect what happens to him. It has occurred to me that perhaps I am an angel now. Could I be a guardian angel? Maybe I am to be Dad's guardian angel; I hope so. But thus far, although I can sense Dad's feelings, I do not think that I have communicated anything to him, or that I have been able to help him at all.

Chapter Four

*T*oday I find Dad sitting alone at his computer, which resides on a table in front of a window facing the lake behind our house. I share his memory of a day, little more than a month before my accident, when he and I sat here for hours playing computer Jeopardy. Playing games that day reminded us of when I was a young girl and we frequently played games; we even discussed those remembrances. Sometime during my teen years, I became too *grown-up* to play those kinds of games with Dad. We did have fun that day, though, and I observe now as he remembers and sheds a tear. I then watch as he erases the Jeopardy game from his computer, knowing that he will never again be able to play the game because it would make him feel too sad.

As he sits, staring out the window, Dad

notices the boat dock, and I feel his memories of seeing me standing down there on the dock one day a few weeks before my accident, talking to one of my friends on our portable phone. I remember that day well. It was two weeks before Christmas, a few inches of snow had fallen the night before, and the lake was frozen over. Ice and snow clung to the tree branches, creating a winter wonderland. In his mind now, Dad sees me, dressed as usual in my denim jeans and jacket, contrasted against the white background of the frozen lake. He watches as I laugh and talk with someone, probably Lynn. I did not know then that Dad was watching me, but now I can feel his intense love for me, a love he must have been feeling that day.

Somehow, Dad and I drifted apart during my teen years. Oh, I know this sounds typical of many teenagers, but in our case, the problem was more severe. It was, of course, mostly my fault. I began to hang out with the wrong crowd, and to experiment with drugs. At first, it was just marijuana, but then I began trying some of the harder stuff. Of course, I blamed

Dad for not understanding me, and for being over-protective. I wish I could tell him now that I understand and that I love him. Somehow, I can feel him telling me these things, but I do not know how I can convey this message to him, or if I will ever be able to let him know. I must believe that he somehow does know, though.

I am *there* a few days later when Dad sells my little Honda bike. This is terribly difficult for him, and tears well up in his eyes as he watches the young girl drive the bike out of the driveway. She does not look at all like me, but as she rides away, the sight of her sitting on the bike, wearing my red helmet, reminds Dad of when he used to watch me leaving to go to work at the ice cream shop. I experience the crying feeling, too, knowing that he is being forced to say goodbye all over again, all so final now. I am glad he sold the bike, though, because I know it made him sad every time he saw it sitting there in the garage. Naturally, I do not want him to forget me, and I know he never will, but neither do I want him to be sad all the time.

I decide to watch over the young girl who now owns the bike, to make sure she understands its little quirks, such as the way the throttle sometimes sticks. I am riding with her now, and as she comes to an intersection, the throttle does stick. She panics, but somehow I make her understand just in time how to fix the problem. I wonder if she was even aware that she had help. Helping people without their knowing about it is fun, I decide, and I begin to wonder if this is what I am meant to do now. Yet, why do I still feel unable to help Dad, the person I most want to help?

Often, I find Dad thinking of me. Not about *me* as I am now, or as I was the last several months of my life, but about the *me* of my earlier growing-up years. I know he wants to remember that bright-eyed little girl, rather than the *me* as I was right before I left him. And I do not blame him for this; I must admit I liked that *me* better, too.

Soon after the accident, Dad put together a picture album. He spent hours searching through drawers, boxes of pictures and photo albums, gathering every picture he could find of me. Then he carefully placed them in chronological order into an album, depicting my life from my birth to my death. The crying feeling overcomes me now as I think about this and about how he intends to share this book with his friends every chance he has.

On a title page in the front of this book, Dad placed a copy of the Memorial Tribute from the funeral home. It contains this poem that I feel is quite appropriate:

> Do not stand at my grave and weep,
> I am not there; I do not sleep.
> I am a thousand winds that blow,
> I am the diamond's gilt on snow.
> I am the sunlight on ripened grain,
> I am the gentle autumn's rain.
> When you awaken in the morning's hush,
> I am the swift uplifting rush
> Of quiet birds in circled flight,
> I am the soft stars that shine at night.
> Do not stand at my grave and cry,
> I am not there; I did *not* die.
>   - Author unknown

Today I find Dad typing something into his computer. I am not sure what he is doing. Perhaps he is writing a book or a journal. I look back at some of the things he has already written.

"February 4, 1990," the writing begins. "I am forty-eight years old and I have just lost my reason for living. My darling Lara has been taken from me, and along with her, my reason for living . . ."

Farther down the page I come across a list of things Dad has written about me, specific little things he wants to remember.

Some random good memories of Lara:

- How exciting she was to be around. Her passion for life was such that she really did *light up* my life, as well as everyone else's life she touched.
- How she enjoyed singing when she was a little girl. She learned every song from the *Sound of Music*, and I loved to hear her sing

those songs. Unfortunately, she stopped singing sometime during her teen years.

- How she always used to know what to give everyone for Christmas. With little money, she was always able to buy some small item that each of us needed or wanted, and it was always thoughtful and appropriate.

- How she so tenaciously urged me to quit smoking that for her tenth birthday present, I did quit. I wonder if she may have saved my life. Ironically, Lara took up smoking as a teenager, although she continually denied it.

- How as a little girl she used to tease me by sneaking up behind me and tickling the hair on my arms or on the back of my neck.

- How she would always stand up for herself, arguing for hours in a good-natured way for whatever she believed.

- How she made so many friends; everyone liked her. Toward the end, I seemed to be the only outsider. Perhaps this was my fault; I was so negative toward her and the lifestyle she had chosen.

- How she loved the little Honda bike that I bought her for her fourteenth birthday when we first moved here. Until the last few months of her life, this was her primary means of getting around.

- How she seemed to enjoy working in the ice cream shop. Sometimes late at night when she came home from work, she would bring me a Banana Split. Sadly, I don't know if I ever remembered to thank her. I suspect that never again will I be able to eat a Banana Split.
- How she hated taking naps as a little girl, always afraid she might miss something, so strong was her zest for life.
- How she was always willing to help anyone in need.
- How much everyone who knew her loved her, especially this grieving father.

I again experience the crying feeling, and I notice tears in Dad's eyes too as he rereads the list, making minor changes. Finally, he is able to continue writing.

"Lara was so much fun to be around. She enjoyed playing games, and was especially good at them, sometimes beating me at Chess, even when she was only nine or ten years old.

She seemed to possess a sixth sense, a sort of psychic ability. I used to joke that I should take her to Las Vegas, for it seemed she could predict and obtain whatever card or dice roll she needed in almost any game of chance. Also extremely adept at games of skill, she possessed an uncanny ability to comprehend the complexities of nearly any game. I taught her to play Bridge before she was ten, although she soon became bored with the game and much preferred games such as Chess, Mastermind or some other board game like Monopoly or Life. We played games frequently during those early years and I miss those times terribly. I miss her so much that I can hardly stand it now; the pain is so much greater than I or anyone could ever have imagined.

"I frequently find myself also thinking now of my darling wife Jeannie, Lara's mother, who was so tragically taken from us years ago at such a young age. Losing Lara, too, now seems more than I can bear, and again I wonder why. Have I so angered God that this is to be my eternal punishment? Lara represented such a part of her mother still with me, my primary physical connection to the love we felt for each other, a love I had always been so certain would never die. Now that I have also lost Lara, what reason is there to go on living? Yet, I somehow know that I must find a way, for what choice have I? Of course, I have considered joining them, but I will not do so now; somehow, I feel that is not my decision to make. For whatever reason, I am destined to go on, somehow to find a way to bear this sorrow; yet, I know not how I will ever find the strength."

The crying feeling overcomes us both as I read Dad's last words and tune in to his thoughts. Sometimes he simply stops whatever he is doing and thinks of some specific event that we shared. Now he is thinking of a time when I was about six years old and we were hiking through a canyon in San Diego, California, our home at the time. Soon after Mom died, Dad, Tracy and I moved to San Diego. We tried to stay busy doing things together in an effort to ease the pain of Mom's death. Dad thinks I may have saved his life that day, because when I noticed that he was about to step on a rattlesnake, I yelled, *SNAKE*, as loudly as I could. Who knows, perhaps I did save his life? He and I will continue to think so, anyway.

Sometimes Dad thinks of things that make me laugh, too, such as when he thinks about how he even misses the *bad* things, such as my messy bedroom and bathroom, and the way I always left my book bag piled on our kitchen table.

"When Lara was ten years old, we moved to northern Virginia. The following year she joined a softball team and I became an umpire for their games. Lara was smaller and not as strong as many of the other girls, but she loved playing softball, and I loved watching her. I will never forget the last game of the season. In the final inning, the score was three to two, Lara's team ahead, the other team batting. The bases were loaded and there were two outs. The batter hit a high fly ball toward Lara's position in the field. She had always had trouble catching fly balls, so we all held our breaths because at least two runs would score and her team would lose the game if she did not catch this ball. The ball miraculously fell into her glove, but she bobbled it and it dropped through her arms. As the ball fell toward the ground, I watched while, as if in slow motion, Lara somehow managed to trap the ball between her knees and hold it. The batter was out! Lara had saved the game. Her teammates carried her off the field on their shoulders that day. This is the Lara I choose to remember."

Dad has finally been able to enter my room and he and Tracy have begun to arrange my things, getting rid of some and packing away others. I am happy as I watch them seal my box of letters and notes. Again, I think of the letter that I wrote to Dad, the one I never gave him. They put all my stuffed animals into another box, including my favorite little brown puppy that I called *Ruggles*. Dad places the boxes in the top of my closet. He looks again at my stereo, wonders about the tape that is still there, and considers pressing the play button. But something prevents him from doing so. He has not yet played the tape, although he noticed it a long time ago. I wonder if he will ever be able to play it. When it is time, I decide. I share his sadness as he again remembers the night of the movie, *Chances Are,* and I *think* a line from the song, *. . . the chances are, your chances are . . . awfully good.*

Not all times were good with Dad, of course, especially during my last two years, when we had more than our share of problems. Since he never seemed to understand me then, I sort of checked out of his life. I only wanted to be with my friends. Dad thought it was because of drugs, and he was partially right, but of course, I never admitted this to him. Finally, I simply gave up trying to make him understand. We shared the same house, but seldom the same life during those final months.

Dad is at his computer again now, continuing to write. Today he writes about some of those bad times and I observe, hoping to find a way to let him know how sorry I am, and that everything is going to be all right now.

Sometimes I have trouble knowing if I am reading his words as he types, or perceiving his thoughts. But it does not matter, for they are mostly the same.

"As difficult as it must be for anyone to lose a child, I sometimes feel that my situation is different," he writes today. "Lara was at an age when many teenagers seem like strangers to their parents, but our situation was more extreme. There were so many unresolved issues between us, and we spent so much of the time over the past two years feeling and showing anger toward one another. For some reason, it seemed that Lara had decided to divorce herself, not only from me, but also from all family. We got to a stage where we seldom did anything together, even including eating meals. When we did talk, the conversation was strained, often resulting in arguments, with each of us becoming angrier than before. I could not help but think that she sometimes purposefully did things she knew would displease me.

"If I am painting a picture of a rebellious and trouble-making teenager, that was not exactly the case. It was not that Lara did bad things so much as she simply did not participate in anything, with the exception of hanging out with her friends. I was never sure what they did, but I suspected it was not all healthy, normal high-school-girl activities. She participated in few school functions, and barely passed some courses, while failing others. Yet, we both knew she could easily have been a straight-A student. I had some concerns that she might not even graduate, although I felt sure she could pull everything out when she had to do so. She proved this during the first six weeks of her senior year when she not only made the honor roll, but the highest honor roll. Naturally, I was proud of her, but with some trepidation because six weeks is such a short time compared to three years of high school. I wish now that I had found more ways to let her know how proud I was of her. The following six-week grades were back to normal, though, barely passing some courses and failing others. It seemed as if she chose not to assume responsibility for anything. She just wanted to have fun and all the privileges, but none of the responsibilities. This is very difficult for me to write, since I am certain this was not the *real* Lara. I have good reason to believe she was involved with drugs or alcohol or both, and that was what controlled her behavior."

You're right, Dad. But it was worse than you think. Well, some of it was, and some was not as bad. I started out just smoking pot with my friends, and I drank a lot of beer, but that was all at first. Then one night this boy I was with—you never even met him—had something he called crack, and I tried it. I was so stupid then. This was right before my sixteenth birthday. He gave me some more the next night too, and the next, and the next. I thought it was awesome. It made me feel better than I had ever felt, and before I knew what was happening, I was hooked. But then they didn't give it to me anymore. Remember, you always asked me what I did with the money I earned working at the ice cream shop. Well, not only that, I stole as much as I could too, just to buy the stuff. You were also right about those missing twenty-dollar bills I lied about not taking from your wallet. I couldn't help myself, Dad. Once I was on it, it had me, and I had to have it.

You were right again when you had that person from the substance abuse center evaluate me. Unfortunately, I was smart enough to convince the counselor that you were wrong, that I didn't have a drug problem. I was as surprised as you were when she told you that she didn't think I had a problem. Of course, by then I had gotten very good at lying—lots of practice, you see. I know you considered putting me into one of those drug rehab places for a few weeks anyway. I felt your pain then and I feel it now, because you couldn't be certain, and if you were wrong, you thought you might drive me away completely.

But Dad, drugs didn't cause the accident. I simply did a stupid thing. I hadn't even had any drugs lately. Perhaps I had two beers the night before, but nothing else. I really was trying to quit, you know. And I would've made it, too. You were right, I was trying to come back, and I know I could have. Who knows, maybe I still can? Too bad I can't do it all over again and make you happy and proud. I wish you could hear this, Dad. I will keep thinking these thoughts and hope someday you will hear me.

"For months I had known all the symptoms were there," Dad continues to write. "Withdrawal, poor grades, avoidance of family, secretive behavior, poor health, skipping school and lies. But I had no evidence indicating what, if anything, Lara might be abusing. I tried to talk with her about it many times, but she always denied using drugs. I know she drank beer, and her best friend, Lynn, told me recently that Lara had a drug problem too, but I was never able to confirm it.

"Regardless, the Lara of old was still there, and sometimes shone through—just not often enough. She seemed to have dug a hole from which she could not escape. And I had no idea what to do. Probably what I did made the problem worse, for mostly all she got from me was negative. When we had a chance to talk, which she made sure was not often, our conversation quickly developed into an argument about what she *should* be doing instead of what she *was*, or *was not*, doing. Much of my sorrow now centers on the anger I felt toward Lara. I could—and should—have been more understanding and accepting. She just had not yet found herself—or perhaps I should say *re-found* herself. And I did not try to help nearly enough. Much more could be said here, but I only want to make clear that Lara and I never had a chance to make peace, and now we never will. That is what makes this loss so much harder for me to endure."

Dad stops writing, as his tears prevent him from seeing the computer screen. I cry with him and plead, *Oh, Dad. Please hear me. PLEASE! It's all right. I'm sorry, too. Please don't give up on me. Chances are we still have a chance.*

Rayford E. Hammond

Chapter Five

I continue to be with Dad nearly all the time; I do not know what else to do. I consider spending some time with my friends, especially Lynn, and one day I go to school for a while. I watch as my old friends go about their lives, but soon I realize they do not need me anymore, not the way that Dad needs me. From what they are saying and doing, and from their thoughts, I can tell that they have been able to let go. They miss me, of course, but they do not need me. They seldom even mention my name, or even think about me at all. But I understand this is how it should be; so, I quickly decide to continue spending my time trying to help Dad, who is still struggling so much. Sometimes he can go for a few hours without thinking of the accident, or thinking of me, but most of the time, especially when he is home alone, this is all he thinks about.

Today I find Dad walking through a shopping mall. As he turns a corner, I feel his sudden shock. He stops, his eyes fixed on someone directly ahead. Then I see her, and I understand. I, too, am taken aback. From Dad's viewpoint, the resemblance is striking. She is walking away from us and from the back, she could be me. This girl is even wearing the same type clothing I usually wore, jeans and a denim jacket, and her hair is about the same length, color and style as mine. She walks exactly the way I did, too, just sort of strolling along.

Dad does not know what to do. He wants to see this girl's face, yet he is afraid. As he cautiously overtakes her, she apparently feels his stare and she stops, turns and looks directly toward him. There is little resemblance in her face, but I know it will be a long time before Dad recovers. The girl gives him a questioning look, then turns and hurries away. I had not thought about the *look-alikes* that might remind Dad of me, but I now realize he may experience similar instances in the future.

Whether this is good or bad I do not know, although perhaps it is something he needs to experience.

Dad is at his computer again now, writing as usual. I think he is looking for some way to be able to let go, and feels that writing about me might help. I read not only what he writes, but also his thoughts. For the most part, they remain the same. I think he is writing down everything he can remember about me.

"The last time I saw Lara was a couple of days before her accident, the night before I left to go to Tracy's. Lara had asked me to go with her to the mall to buy her some new shoes. Afterwards, as we were heading back toward the car, a strange thing happened. As we walked through the parking lot, I felt Lara's hand in mine. She thanked me for buying her the shoes, and right before we got into the car, she hugged me. This would not have been so unusual for Lara prior to about age fourteen, but it was not at all like her during the past several months. At the time, I did not think too much about it, but as I look back now, I wonder if she might have known even then that she would never see me again."

I have to think for a while about what Dad has just written. Could I have known then, as he said? Not consciously, of course, but might I have had some subconscious indication that I would never see him again?

"There are many events that make me think that Lara might have been aware of her fate, particularly during the past year. But I am in no position to make that judgment, so I will try to think about this in other terms. I remember her primarily as that bright-eyed, happy little girl who had such a contagious curiosity about life. So exceptionally bright, she never ceased to amuse everyone with her quick wit and charming personality. She was the light and the delight of my life for the first fourteen years of her life; yet, she was the greatest concern of my life during her last two years.

"When Lara was twelve years old, we moved back to California, and she seemed the happiest then that I had ever seen her. She was going back to the land of her childhood, where she still had many friends, and would be returning to her same school she had left two years before. We celebrated when we crossed the California stateline, and I even allowed Lara to steer our station wagon across the line into California. Then I took a picture of her standing by the *Welcome to California* sign. That picture now has a special place in my *Lara* album. Life seemed the best we had ever known it then. When we arrived in California, we bought a new house, installed a swimming pool and had a great time for a couple of years.

"Lara's graduation from junior high school was a major event. She and a few of her girl friends rented a stretch limo and rode around San Diego for hours the night after graduation. Shortly after this event, I began to realize I might not want to stay in California. There were many reasons, but the most significant was that I thought it might be good to get Lara away from the fast life, the drug scene, and take her to a small-town environment, similar to where I had grown up. I find it ironic now that in this environment is where she likely became more involved with drugs, and eventually lost her life. But I must not continue to play *what-if* with my decision. It is too difficult, for I still blame myself. *What if* I had done things differently?

"Lara did not want to leave California when I forced her to move away. She could not understand why I would even consider leaving, how I could do that to her, especially since she was about to enter high school. We moved here during the summer before she was to begin tenth grade. After about a month of fighting it, Lara adjusted quickly and made many new friends at her new school in this small town situated in the Cumberland Mountains of Tennessee. I learned how quickly she had begun to love it here when we returned to California for Christmas, only a few months after moving away. By then, I had decided that perhaps I had made a mistake leaving California, and was considering moving back. I intended to give Lara a Christmas present: the opportunity to move back to San Diego. When I told her, she cried. She did not want to leave our small town. From that time on, she refused even to discuss leaving, and toward the end, even had I left, she probably would have remained here to finish high school. I, however, did not like the lifestyle she had adopted, and wanted to get her away from it any way I could. Although I promised her that we would stay until she graduated, I still listed the house on the market, and had it sold, we might have left. Again, *what-if?*

"But I only want to remember the good times, which, of course, is difficult since I am still living in this house where I have so many memories of *not-so-good* times. Not everything was bad here, of course, but there were more bad times than good. So many nights when Lara was out (which was nearly every night), I lay in bed dreading the phone call. I sometimes feel that I dreaded it so much that I may have caused it. I would not have been surprised to receive a phone call in the middle of the night that Lara had been involved in an automobile accident. But I was surprised when the call came at nine o'clock in the morning on that clear, sunny day, informing me that she had been killed in an accident on the way to school.

"Although I'd had many concerns about Tracy during her teenage years, and thought I had experienced nearly every problem, things never seemed as bad then as during these last months here with Lara. Having often caught her in lies, I did not feel I could trust her. She was not doing the things I felt she should be doing, and I was afraid of finding out what she might be doing. Some of her friends seemed normal, but many were not the type people with whom I thought she should be associating. They were not necessarily bad, but some were high school dropouts, with no jobs and little concern for what they were going to do. Most of them smoked, drank, and who knows what else? Nearly everyone in town in Lara's age range, from fifteen through twenty-one, seemed to be her friend. More than two hundred showed up at her funeral, which was remarkable in such a small town.

"The only way I was able to cope with the situation was simply to turn off my feelings, almost assuming a *don't-care* attitude. My emotional health was not very good then, and certainly is no better now, which seems odd, because after the accident my friends all told me how well they thought I was handling everything. And it seemed so to me, at first. I tried to do all the right things: experience the grief, release emotions, talk about my feelings, and not try to escape. I did, however, visit California for a few days to see my friends there and again to experience many of the places that held such good memories of Lara. Then I came back here and experienced these feelings and memories in this empty house.

"I am here now. Not that I want to be here, but for some reason the house has not yet sold, so perhaps I am meant to remain here for a while longer. But I think it is time to leave. When I am away from here, I can sometimes get through two or three hours without thinking of Lara and the accident. But when I am here, not fifteen minutes pass that I do not relive some event concerning Lara. I do not want her memory ever to fade, but I want to remember our good times and not always be reminded of the bad times. I have many regrets concerning the emotions that I experienced here, the anger I felt much of the time, and I do not want to be constantly reminded of that.

"A specific memory I have is of one morning when I was taking Lara to school during the early weeks of her senior year. I had again received a notice to see the principal about Lara's repeated absences from school. A few of these absences I knew about, but many I did not. On our way to school that morning, we were having our standard argument about the usual subject: Lara's lack of participation and responsibility, and her unconcerned attitude about school, family and so on. I made a statement that although it was a terrible thing to say, the primary memory I might have of her entire high school days would be these visits to the principal to get her out of trouble. When I left her at school that morning, she was crying. I wanted to talk with her about it, but was on my way to a business appointment and she was late for class, so we never talked. I cried nearly all the way to my destination that morning. Every time I think about it now, I regret having said those things. I want to tell her now how sorry I am, although I thought at the time that what I said was true."

Dad, I knew you did not mean what you said. But I also knew that it was true. I know I caused you so much grief, and I wish I could do it all over again, only this time I would do things differently. Will you ever understand how sorry I am? Please, please hear me. Please know how much I love you. And please, Dad, do not feel guilty. You have to get on with your life. Don't let my accident control you forever. I am fine. I love you. Please hear me.

Rayford E. Hammond

Chapter Six

I feel a need to leave now to contemplate all the things Dad has written. I call it leaving, although I do not think I actually go any place different. I simply place myself into a state of aloneness, apart from the physical. This seems so strange, and is, of course, impossible to describe. The closest thing I can think of would be like going to sleep or into a trance, although when in this state I remain fully aware—perhaps even more so. This feels somewhat like watching yourself from a distance during a dream.

Although I am seemingly alone when away from the physical, I do not feel alone. I sense some presence, but I have not yet encountered another being. If *here* is a place, then I suppose I have not yet been able to manifest myself fully into it, as if I have not yet become part of this new dimension. I must continue to pursue this question, where is *here*.

It seems as if a long time has passed since my accident, as time is measured *there*, in the physical dimension that I continue to inhabit so much of the time. When I direct my consciousness toward this new dimension or state of being, wherever I am now, I feel tremendous peace and profound love. It seems I have recently awakened *here* and the time that has passed, assuming any time has passed at all, seems like only seconds. I have begun to feel a need to explore this place, assuming it is a place, but I do not yet know how.

Everything still feels like a dream, as if this is all taking place in my mind, although these sensations are much stronger and I somehow know this is real. I can feel *me, Lara*, and I am aware that I am different from before; yet, in many respects I feel the same. There is no physical feeling, of course, and I have begun to wonder if perhaps this is the major difference *here*—that in this dimension, I feel no physical needs.

As I think more about this subject, I begin

to realize that the satisfaction of physical needs consumes a major portion of our time and effort while in the physical body. Actually, it seems these needs take up nearly all of our time. Eating, sleeping, resting, exercising, bathing, sex, providing clothing and shelter, along with the preparation for all these activities, such as the gathering and cooking of food, use up nearly all of our time and energy while *there*. And if we become sick or injured, then we must expend even more time and effort with the physical needs. Since I have no physical needs *here*, I seem to have lots more free time, and I am not yet sure what I am to do.

Recently I made another amazing discovery: the laws of nature that we take for granted in the physical world do not seem to apply in this dimension. Since I have no physical body, I have no weight, and as gravity does not affect me, I feel free to move about with no encumbrances to impede my movement from place to place. Physical walls or barriers do not prevent my passage either, and it seems that no time transpires between leaving one place and arriving at another, no matter how far the distance. I assume I can go anywhere, although I have barely explored this concept. Another difference is that since I have no physical body, I never feel tired, have no need of sleep, and I can concentrate all my energy on nonphysical things.

It occurs to me that others whose state is similar to mine, whatever that might be, must also occupy this space or dimension. Almost as soon as I experience this realization, I begin to sense another being. Something unusual is happening, almost as if someone has entered my space. The feeling is similar to being alone and sensing that someone is watching, except that this sensation feels much stronger. I am not afraid, though; I feel only love.

Uncertain what to do, I *think* a question: *Is someone here?*

Almost immediately I receive a response, which if put into words would translate as *Yes, Lara, I am here.* I suppose I must somehow have received this message through my subconscious.

Then suddenly another transmission finds

its way into my consciousness: *Welcome, Lara. It is time you begin to learn about where you are and why you are here.*

The awesomeness of this aura I feel surrounding me is overwhelming. I must be dreaming; yet, this feels so real. I try to respond, to *think* some of my many questions, and they all come at once. *Why can't I see you? Are you real? Should I be glad to be here? Where is here?* What *is here? Is this Heaven? Who are you? How long have I been here?*

I feel a sense of gaiety, almost as if the source of this strange communication is laughing. Then another message enters my consciousness: *You must have many questions, Lara. Almost everyone does. As you think your questions, I will try to answer them. You must understand, however, that you are not yet ready to comprehend certain things, so for questions relating to these things, you must simply have patience.*

First, am I real? *Of course—although perhaps not as you are yet able to comprehend.*

Should you be glad to be here? *Yes, you*

are precisely where you belong, where you have always been, since the beginning of time.

Is this Heaven? *No, not as you probably think of Heaven.*

Who am I? *My name in the physical realm was Mioki, so you may call me that name now if you wish. You must understand, however, that I am much more than Mioki. I am all I have ever been and all I ever will be, although this must also be beyond your comprehension now, just as is the concept that you are much more than Lara. When you are drawn into the light, you will be able to understand all these things.*

How long have you been here? *I should probably first explain that the concept of time is different here. Perhaps you have already noticed this. Based on your concept of time, you have been here for a few weeks. However, time is of no consequence here; there is no need to measure time, and it would be meaningless anyway when compared with eternity. Perhaps in your concept of time you may feel as if you have only been here for a few seconds.*

Again, welcome, Lara. We have been feeling your presence and waiting until you were ready to experience us.

Apparently, Mioki—what a strange, yet beautiful name—feels there is so much I am not yet ready to comprehend—and is she ever right about that! I can only stammer, *I—I don't know what to say. I still have so many other questions. And you didn't really tell me where we are. And you just said "ready to experience us, Mioki." What exactly do you mean by* us?

You must understand that we are many here, Lara; but you will communicate only with me for a while. Otherwise, things might seem too confusing to you, with so much energy invading your consciousness all at once. You may think of me as your spiritual guide. I will assist you to adapt to your new transcendental state. As for where we are, I suppose this does not match any of your preconceived notions, does it?

That's for sure!

Perhaps I can explain, Lara. You see, whenever someone dies, as you call the transformation, they first come here. Here *is not a place, however—not as you comprehend a physical place. But since we are not physical here, we, of course, have no need of a place, such as in the physical dimension. If you must continue to feel that you are in a place, then believe that you are where you were—where you always have been and always will be, actually. Soon you will no longer feel this need to be in a physical place. I realize this must seem somewhat confusing, but that is partially because you are choosing to remain attached to the physical. Even now, you still sense your previous physical surroundings, although no one in that dimension can see or hear you. They may occasionally sense your presence, as if you are entering or possibly even influencing their thoughts, but they do not know you are still there.*

Wow! This is so rad, Mioki. Are you saying that we are here *and* there *at the same time? Or that* here *is* there*? I'm sorry, I just—*

Mioki's response immediately manifests itself in my consciousness. *Yes, the physical place is the same, but as we are only spiritual here, this is difficult at first to comprehend.*

Do not try to understand everything so soon, Lara. You need not be in such a hurry.

Okay. Mioki, are you an angel?

If by angel you mean a guardian celestial spirit or guiding influence, then yes, you may think of me as an angel. You may have noticed that you, too, already possess some angelic-like traits, such as an ability to change locations instantaneously, much as you think of moving from place to place. Only after you are more spiritually enlightened, however, will you be able to comprehend the real meaning and significance of angels.

Spiritually enlightened? *What do you mean by* enlightened? *Are you saying that somehow I will understand all this the way you understand it, Mioki?*

Yes, of course you will, Lara, but only when you are ready to accept it. As long as you choose to cling to the physical, as you are now doing, then you will resist moving toward the light. You will feel more drawn in that direction, though, as your concept of time passes here.

The Light? *You mean—are you saying that*

there really is a light—I mean, like we hear about when someone dies—I mean nearly dies—and comes back claiming they saw some bright light that was drawing them toward it? I never really believed all that was true. Is that what you mean by the light, *Mioki?*

Not exactly. You still think of seeing light with your eyes. Here we see in a different way, which you must already have experienced to some extent. Lara, look at me.

Look at you? I cannot see you, Mioki. I mean, we are, uh, dead, aren't we? If we're dead, then we must be out of our physical body. So how would I be able to see you, Mioki?

Of course, you cannot physically see *me, as you think of seeing, but do you not sense my presence, Lara? Look toward where you perceive that I am and tell me what you feel— what you sense or perceive—or see if you want to call it that.*

I . . . well, it is hard to describe. But then I guess I don't need to describe it to you, do I? I see—or I sense—some sort of a glow, but it is dim. I feel drawn toward it, though, and I feel tremendous love. Is that what you mean,

Mioki? Am I supposed to go toward this light now?

When it is time, my child—when you are ready. I must first explain some other things to you, things about what you call life. You see, Lara, your life as you think of it is far from over. Life is so much more than people in the physical state are able to comprehend. In reality, your life has hardly even begun, although of course, you have already lived forever.

Now Mioki, you have to explain that better! I mean, how can I be dead, but my life still be far from over? And yet, you say I have already lived forever? This is all too confusing.

I know it seems that way, Lara, but it is all very simple. What actually happens when you die probably does not exactly match many of the theories that have developed regarding what you call this transition from the physical to the spiritual. You must first understand that the physical Lara is not you, *as I am sure you have already begun to comprehend. You, the entity, are so much more than merely the physical Lara. It is now time to begin to get to know the spiritual Lara. Do you understand?*

Yes, I think so—sort of. But Mioki, what about God? You have not mentioned Him. Can you tell me about God? I mean—assuming of course that He exists.

You already know that God exists, Lara—although perhaps not in the way that you and many people believe. You see, simply stated, God is Love. *The Bible affirms this frequently; yet for some reason, people continue trying to invent their own version of God. Perhaps you can better understand if you think of God as the* source *of love. Of course, God is the source of everything: all power, all knowledge, all energy, all life. Every living thing is a part of God and God is part of everything. Therefore, God is everything, and everything is God. Each part contains* all *the components of the whole, yet the part is not the whole. Are you able to understand this concept, Lara?*

Uh, I think so . . . but I'm not sure.

Think of a drop of water. Does it not contain all the ingredients of water, just as does a bucket of water or an ocean of water? Yet each small amount of water is simply a part of the whole, possessing all the elements of the whole; yet, the part is not *the whole. You see, God exists in you, Lara, in what you call your soul—much as I am there now, for you cannot see me either, although I think you believe that I exist.*

I am overwhelmed as Mioki continues to explain. Mostly I just listen now, trying to understand.

We are closer to God here, Lara, meaning that we feel more love and we have access to more knowledge and power—all knowledge and power, actually, but you could not absorb this all at once. Have you noticed already that you no longer retain any of your previous negative feelings or emotions, such as resentments, grudges, hateful feelings, or feelings of revenge that might have controlled you while in your physical body?

Yes, Mioki, I have noticed that.

You feel primarily only love now, such as the love you feel for your father. No longer do you retain any of the anger or misunderstanding that often dominated you while there. And the longer you are here, the more love, joy and understanding you will experience, as you move closer to God, back into the whole. This is, of course, what moving toward the light means. The closer you get, the more you will understand and the more love you will feel. So do not worry, my child, everything will become clear when it is time. You need not be concerned now, as long as you continue to learn, for learning is one of our primary purposes, both here and there.

Okay, but I've been wondering about something else, Mioki. Is there any way I can communicate with someone in the physical state? I mean, just to tell them that I love them, or to help them understand that I am all right, and that they can go on with their life.

Nearly everyone has this question, Lara. There are ways, but not in the sense that you mean, and you are not yet ready to learn many of these methods. Sometimes we employ intermediaries—those who have more power or more ability to communicate. These methods are unusual, though, and are primarily reserved for extreme cases. Your case is not at all unusual or extreme, Lara. But where there is an unresolved issue, such as with your physical father, more association is often permitted with the physical realm. You may spend as much time there now as you wish, although practically no time, as you understand the concept, will pass here while you are there. You must remember, though, that the time you choose to spend there will delay your transition into the light or the whole.

Wow!

I know this is a little difficult to comprehend, Lara, but you will find that those loved ones who miss you will soon begin to go on with their lives. This is how it is meant to be. They must release you, just as you must release them. They will never forget you in that you will continue to live in their hearts; but they must eventually let you go—the physical you, just as you must let them go. It is good that you cannot communicate with them, for that would only make things more difficult, both for them and for you, as it would delay the release even more. Rarely does anyone here ever communicate directly with someone in the physical state. You can understand how that could be disastrous. There are ways to help those who are still in the physical without their knowing about it, though, as I am sure you must have already experienced.

Yes, but only in little things. It feels so good, though . . . and I don't even want them to know I'm helping.

I decide to tell Mioki about the girl on my motor bike and how I thought I helped prevent her from crashing, and Mioki agrees that I probably did help her.

Are we sort of like guardian angels here, Mioki?

No, not exactly. Guardian angels are often assigned to help a particular person, usually on a full-time basis. They are assigned full-time only to those who really need them, though, such as a person born with a physical handicap, retardation for example, who needs someone to watch over them for their entire time while in the physical state. Nearly everyone needs a guardian angel sometimes, though, and when those times occur, an angel will appear. Often in the physical state, we may feel as if some divine inspiration has intervened, and that is exactly what happens. A guardian angel comes to us in our times of need. Unfortunately, some do not believe, and therefore refuse to recognize the existence of these angels, which means they miss receiving the help that is available. We here are able to help sometimes in that manner, too, but not nearly so much as the assigned angels.

Wow! That is awesome . . . but it sure sounds complicated.

It is not nearly so complicated as it may seem at first. All this is difficult to explain without your comprehending the subject of eternity, which of course you cannot yet grasp. Perhaps I can simplify things for you. If eternity is forever—think of it as the mathematical term, infinity—then the time an individual spends there is so short in relation to eternity as to be inconsequential. This is why the concept is so confusing to people while in the physical state. It seems to them as if they are there for a long time, in their concept of time; yet, seventy, a hundred, or even thousands of years are not even measurable in terms of eternity. Remember, the Bible refers to a day as being like a thousand years, in relation to eternity, of course.

All I can think to say is *wow* or *awesome*, which I have already said repeatedly, so I just remain quiet and listen, trying to absorb all that Mioki is telling me.

Contrary to what some believe, Lara, accidents do happen. Unanticipated turns of events occur, based primarily on the fact that we have free will and we make mistakes. This is, of course, how we learn. Sometimes these mistakes even cause us to depart the physical dimension before completing our tasks there. A person's time there might even end much too soon, such as in your case. Our eternity, however, is not determined by our immeasurably short time in the physical state, as many believe, nor does a single mistake cause our eternity to be altered. Only when we are ready do we continue to another plateau. So, as I said, what you call life is so much more than you are yet able to comprehend. Your subconscious mind stores or remembers everything that has happened to you since the beginning of time. Actually, it also has access to everything that is to happen in the future, but for most, this is far too frightening to experience. I know this must seem different from how you were taught, Lara, but actually, it is not so different as you might think. Everything fits perfectly into the grand design, if people would but open their minds to the possibilities.

Do you have any more questions now, Lara? Ask and I will answer if I can. Remember, though, you must not try to understand everything so soon. You have plenty of time.

Uh, okay, Mioki . . . but just one more thing. I guess I somehow know that I am still me, *and I sort of understand that I always have been and I always will be, although I'm not sure how I know this. So, are you saying that our subconscious remembers or has access to everything?*

Yes, Lara, something like that. We do not consciously remember certain things, such as the characteristics we possess when in the physical state, yet we are still the same entity, the same person we have always been and always will be. Your soul is eternal, Lara. The closer you approach to the light, the clearer all these things will seem. Even in the physical state, the subconscious has the ability to access all knowledge and to communicate with the whole or with God. This part of us has the ability to draw from the omniscient and omnipotent source.

Mioki has lost me now, so I decide to change the subject, hoping she will not detect my ineptness. Of course, I suppose she is aware of everything I am thinking, anyway.

Yes, Lara, I do know your thoughts—but do not be concerned. You will only experience pure thoughts here, so you need have no fear.

Okay, but I just thought of another question now, okay?

All right, but only this one more now.

Okay. I don't quite know how to ask this, but I've been wondering about church and religion, things like that. It all seems so confusing. I guess most people do wonder *about this, especially when they get close to leaving there. Anyway, there are so many churches and religions, and people get so hung up on their particular beliefs. How do we know which is right? Or does it matter? What if I did not go to church often—or at all—or what if I went to the wrong one?*

These are questions that nearly everyone eventually asks. I will try to clear this up for you. First, which is right and does it matter? *The simple answer is: nearly all, almost none, and not necessarily.*

Sensing my perplexed state, Mioki begins to explain even before I have time to ask.

I am sorry, Lara, I will explain. People invented religion primarily to help them deal with their mortality—or immortality—they are not always certain which. Religion provides something beyond one's physical being on which to base a reason for living. My response of nearly all *means that most religions are right about some things, as far as they go, and their intent is usually good. By* almost none, *I mean that no single set of beliefs contains all the answers. Finally, our eternity is* not necessarily *determined by which, if any, religion we choose to espouse.*

Now, about the concept of church. First, do not confuse church and religion, or church and spiritualism, or church and Godliness. These may or may not be related. And as for which church one attends, including none at all, it does not particularly matter. God is within us, Lara, wherever we are. Sometimes being in a particular church brings us no closer to God than being any place else; perhaps some churches even push people farther from God. Now, do not misunderstand; the concept *of church is good. Many people simply attend for the wrong reasons. Some churches also do more harm than good, primarily by instilling unwarranted feelings of guilt, which is one of the most destructive manmade emotions. Some religions, through guilt, cause people to do the wrong things for the right reasons, or the right things for the wrong reasons, each equally destructive.*

What is important, Lara, is that which is in your heart. Our own personal association with God is all that matters. If a particular church or religion helps one to form and maintain that association, then it may be good. Sometimes being with others who are concerned with forming and maintaining a close association with their God can be good, too. But this is not necessary and has little to do with what happens throughout our life journey.

You will have many opportunities to learn the things you must learn before moving on to the next plateau. Do not forget that we have forever. So there is no need to worry about whether you did or did not attend a particular church during one phase of your journey. God knows what is in your heart, for He too is there, regardless of whether you ever attended a church. Remember that in many parts of the world there are no churches. Certainly, people there must still have some means of communicating with God. Does this help you to understand, Lara?

I guess so, Mioki, but now I have another question.

Yes, my child, but this must be the last one for now.

Okay, I promise. I guess you already know about Dad, I mean what he's doing . . .what he's going through. Is there any way I can let him know I understand, and that I'm okay? I know I've asked this already, but either you did not answer or I did not understand your response.

I think he already knows, Lara. Do you not sometimes feel that he senses you still exist? I think you do.

Yes, sometimes I think I can, but I'm not sure. Are we ever sure, Mioki?

In the long term perhaps, although not necessarily at first. You will get there, Lara; do not give up.

Okay. But now there's just one other thing that I have to ask. Okay? Please?

All right, Lara, but this must definitely be the last one.

Okay, I promise. My question is, when we are there and about to come here—I mean before we're about ready to leave, like maybe some weeks before—do we ever know? I do not mean consciously, but does our subconscious or our soul sort of sense that we are going to be departing soon and maybe this causes us to act differently?

If I understand you correctly, Lara, what you are asking is this: do you have any forewarning that you are about to leave the physical state?

Yes, that is what I mean. Dad seems to think I might have had some indication that I was leaving, and that this could explain why I acted the way I did. He thinks, for example, that may have been the reason I held his hand and hugged him that night a couple of days before the accident, almost as if I knew then that I might never see him again. Does that kind of thing ever happen?

Sometimes, but usually only when one is physically old there. I do not think this happened in your case, Lara. You simply had an accident. We seldom consciously know when we are about to leave the physical, but of course our inner self, or our soul, is always aware of when it is time to go. Does that answer your question?

Yes, I guess so . . . sort of. You make everything seem so simple, Mioki. I know it is not, and I know you are not telling me everything, but thanks for helping.

You are most welcome, Lara. And you are correct that I am not telling you everything. As I said, some things must be experienced, as you will when it is time. Do not worry so much now. Everything tends to work out exactly as designed, if we will only allow things to take their course. Events occur in cycles, and in time everything balances out, or comes back anew, much like the old cliché: what goes around comes around.

Although I still have hundreds of questions, Mioki says I must rest now and allow the things she has told me to be absorbed and cogitated for a while. Some things are at the same time both clearer and more confusing, because each question Mioki answered generated even more questions. I want to know everything immediately, but I understand how that cannot be. Besides, I feel a need to get back to Dad. Something significant could be happening *there*, and he might need my help.

Chapter Seven

*H*aving come out of my dreamlike state now, I find myself back with Dad—assuming that I ever left. If only I had all the answers for him. I do have some—certainly more than before—but even if I knew all the answers, how could I tell him? Again, I experience the crying feeling as I think of what I must have put him through. Of course, I did not mean to do it, and I did not think things were so bad at the time. But then I was so involved in my own self-interests, concerned about hardly anything or anyone other than myself. Dad also put me through a lot, but I guess he never knew that either. I so wish we could talk about it now. I suppose this is what Dad is saying, that he wishes we could have another chance to make things right. I know now that I *must* find a way as Dad continues his writing and I experience it with him.

"One of the last good times Lara and I shared was during the latter part of 1989, only a few weeks before her accident. We decided to go to a movie together, which was a rare event for us in those days. That night we saw a movie called *Chances Are,* and we became emotionally caught up in it. The movie was about a man who got killed and then came back as another person to try to make things right. Sometimes I wonder what drew us to see that particular movie, and why we were so moved by it. We shared some feelings that night that we had not shared in a long time. I remember two songs from the movie. One was called *Chances Are,* by Johnny Mathis, which had already been a favorite of mine. The other was a song I had not heard before that night, recorded by Cher and Peter Cetera, called *After All.* Strangely, we heard that song on the radio during our trip home from the theater that night. Lara bought the tape the next day and she played the song repeatedly. I found the tape in her tape player a few days after the accident. It is still there, where it will probably remain, but I have not yet been able to play the song, and do not know if I ever will.

"I chose the song, *Chances Are*, to be played at Lara's funeral, which probably seemed strange to almost everyone there. But it meant something to me, and I hope to Lara, even if no one else understood. I somehow feel she did understand. That song represents one of our final good times together, and one of the few times during the past several months when Lara and I shared anything positive. It also speaks of how I feel about her.

"Another song I chose for the service was *Smoke Gets In your Eyes*. The words, *When a lovely flame dies, smoke gets in your eyes*, just about say it all. And my *lovely flame* has died. I picked this particular song partially because of another movie entitled *Always,* a movie that Lara never saw. Tracy and I saw the movie the night before Lara's accident, and I knew that Lara would have liked it. I had intended to take her to see that movie when I returned home the following day. The night of Lara's funeral, I, along with some other members of our immediate family, saw the movie again, but I am not sure how much it meant to them. I know some did not understand, but that does not matter. Hearing either of these two songs will forever bring tears to my eyes because they remind me of how much I love and miss Lara. I doubt anyone could ever understand how I feel when I hear these songs."

Except me, Dad. ME, Lara. I understand. PLEASE hear me, Dad.

"There are times when I still do not believe she is really gone. I suppose I am still in the denial phase. Frequently, late at night, I expect to hear the front door open, just as usual. Sometimes she would get home a few minutes past her curfew, but she always had a good excuse for being late. When she knew she was going to be late, she would usually stop and call to tell me she was on her way home, and not to worry. She was very good about calling, and I wish now that I had told her more often how much I appreciated that. Sometimes I still expect the phone to ring. I will answer, it will be Lara and she will say, *Hi, Dad. I'm on my way home. Didn't want ya to worry about me. See ya in a few minutes. Love ya,*

Bye. Naturally, I find myself cringing now every time the phone rings.

"During my bad times, I dwell on the fact that the accident proves bad things can happen to me, and I look for other bad things that must be coming my way. Fortunately, those times are not every day anymore, but they still occur much too frequently. I would give anything, including my own life, to have Lara back. But I know, or strongly believe, that she is not really gone; she is just in another stage of life, somewhere beyond my ability to comprehend."

He KNOWS! He really KNOWS! Maybe I have been getting through to him. Oh, Dad, I wish I could talk with you now. I miss you so much and I know you miss me, too. Please know that everything is all right. I'm simply here, waiting for whatever comes next. Things are good here. Great, actually. But so different from how you or anyone else there could imagine. And I don't feel dead at all. I'm just no longer in that physical body.

It seems Dad might be hearing me now, so

I pause to allow him to continue his writing. I observe closely to see if he thinks anything that might suggest he got my message. I notice Dad has the radio playing, tuned as usual to his favorite easy listening oldies station. He and I are both surprised as the song, *Lara's Theme*, from the movie, *Doctor Zhivago*, begins playing. Dad has always associated this song with my name, Lara, and as he hears the words: *Somewhere my love, there will be songs to sing* . . . tears flood his eyes. He stands and walks across the room to the table in the corner where he has placed my senior class picture. He stares at the image, looking into my dark brown eyes, and I can almost feel his sensation that I am looking back at him as he whispers the words: "Somewhere, my love . . ."

After a few moments, he returns to his computer and continues writing. "I cannot know if I shall ever see Lara again—probably not in a way that my physical senses can perceive. I doubt there has ever been any communication across the dimensions, or whatever separates us, yet on the other hand, sometimes I do feel her presence. And one of those times is now. Perhaps my mind is simply creating what I want to be, but that does not matter, for I can feel it.

"All I know for sure is that I do not know anything for sure anymore. I have reevaluated every belief I held, and have not yet come to terms with what I now believe. Perhaps I never shall, but I can sometimes let it go now, which I was unable to do before beginning this writing. Sometimes I do not have to know *why* anymore; I can simply accept things as they are. Tracy and I talk frequently about this subject, and she has helped me to accept that I do not have to understand everything. Andy and I talk a lot too. He does not know what to say, but just having him around and knowing that he cares means so much to me. I should tell him that the next time I see him.

"For a long time after the accident, I was disturbed because I did not feel anger. In fact, I sometimes felt relief. Often I wondered what worse thing could happen. Obviously, if I could get through this, then I could handle any of the less important things that might come my way. Only during the past few weeks have

I begun to feel angry. This is not anger toward any particular person or thing. I simply sometimes find myself angry, primarily because the accident happened, I suppose. Obviously, I cannot change anything. Life must go on, and no matter what *could* have been, I must go on to what *will* be.

"Another part of my feelings has to do with the fact that I lost Lara long before the accident. I had already experienced so much grief before her death, because I felt as if she had gone away long ago. I often wondered what happened to that bright-eyed little girl I had so enjoyed being around. Yes, Lara left me long before she left this final time. The difference is, there was some hope that she would return, and sometimes it seemed as if she might be trying to come back. I do not know if that would have ever happened, but I choose to think it would have. Even so, sometimes I believe the lifestyle she had chosen was certain to have caused her years of grief. I think she would have had to work so hard to recover, if she ever could have, and I sometimes feel that what happened might not be as bad as it could have been. But who am I to make this judgment? I still struggle with the fact that I had already experienced so much grief before the accident, wondering what I had done to cause my little girl to go away. I may never know, and I must now live with that uncertainty; I have no other choice. There were so many times when I tried to talk with Lara about this subject, but we were never able to resolve anything.

"I doubt that Lara knew herself. It just happened. Several of her family members voiced their concern during the past year, sometimes in the form of letters from her sister, her uncle and her cousins. Lara never mentioned the effect, if any, of these letters. Her attitude seemed to be, *just leave me alone; I don't want to talk about this; I just want to live my life the way I want to live it.* Could she have known that she had no need to prepare for the future? I do not choose to believe this, but I cannot rule out the possibility either.

"The time has now come to forget the bad things, to catalog the good, and to get on with my life. I choose to think that when this house sells and I can continue with whatever I decide to do with the rest of my life, things will be different. I realize they may not be, though. I find myself bored much of the time, with far too much time to think about what happened, to play *what-if*, to ask the *why* questions, and to blame myself. Will things ever be easier? Surely, time will heal, as they say it does.

"I will never be the same, though. Lara will forever be a part of me, and a part of me died with her. I hope she was happy, and I trust she knew how very much I loved her. I hope she knows how much I love and miss her now. Sometimes, though, I feel I am being selfish. Do I want her back for her sake or for mine? Do I miss her so much because I feel guilty for not having let her know how much I loved her? I had thought frequently about what might happen to Lara to help her find herself. Sometimes I even anticipated an automobile accident; I just never expected that she would be killed.

"I still sometimes have the feeling that *this cannot be*. And often I wonder if the accident happened as a punishment for me. I feel that I sometimes create things, and often wonder if I created her accident. Frequently I ask the question: How can I live with myself if I did cause this? Tracy tells me that I might be able to create things in my life, but that I could not have caused or prevented Lara's accident. Although I try to believe her, and I want to believe her, I still wonder. I will probably never get past the question, *Why did this happen*? I can only decide that I do not have to know the answer.

"I wish I could tell Lara now how much I love her and miss her. Perhaps in a way that is exactly what I am doing. Maybe this writing was necessary for me so that I could turn loose and create another type of relationship that I can live with from here on. All I know is that while writing this I have cried a lot, and I have spent much time with a lump in my throat. Why does this have to be so final?"

Oh Dad, you did *tell me you love me, just now. I only wish you could know for sure that I heard you. Actually, I think you do know, but I just wish I could tell you. It means so much to me to know how you feel, though, and how you felt—even including the bad things. I will let you know, somehow, some way. Watch for me in your dreams. Don't give up on me.*

As Dad continues his attempt to write about his feelings, I want to share everything with him. For some reason, I think he might complete his writing today.

"I think I could answer this question, *where do I go from here,* even before discussing it, and the answer would likely be the same as it will when I finish: *I don't know.* With that in mind, however, I shall attempt to write about it in an effort to show that I have spent some time thinking about this issue. I do not expect an answer to miraculously appear as I write, but if it does, I will attempt to write it down.

"I am still waiting for someone to come along and buy the house. Perhaps this will happen soon. Just today two couples came by and looked at the house. Both seemed to like it, but no offer yet. I have made no firm decision where I will go, what I will do, or how I will choose to live when I can leave here. All I know is that I am ready to go. I will most likely have no difficulty making this decision when the time comes. As for now, the most likely place is California, since that is where I have the fondest memories of Lara. I do not want to leave my friends here, especially Andy and Tracy, who have helped me so much, but somehow I know that leaving is what I need. Although I feel the time is near, this does not make it easier for me to have patience to wait. I seem to be simply waiting to get on with the rest of my life, whatever and wherever it may be.

"The question, *where do I go from here*, means, of course, much more than where I will physically live. More importantly, it has to do with what I will do with the rest of my life. Where I go may be a factor, but what I do is of more importance. I know, for example, that going some place else will not necessarily change anything, but the move from here will mark the beginning of a new way of life, a life I am hesitant to start until I leave here. Perhaps I am placing too much importance on location and not enough on the issue of *how* to live the rest of my life, but I cannot seem to do anything differently now.

"I feel that I need a purpose or a goal. I seem to be happy only when I have a challenge, yet at the same time, I do not want the pressure and stress of too many difficulties. Nothing is important enough to worry too much about; on the other hand, I find myself concerned about any little thing that does not go the way I think it should. If I can let go, then possibly I can grow from this experience, but if I continue to blame myself, then I could also go in the other direction. I often wonder if anything will ever be fun again. Will I become interested in doing anything new? It seems that a phase of my life has ended and the next phase has yet to begin. Meanwhile time passes, I get older, and the rut deepens. I know I must soon again become involved with the human race, the life race, or it will be over.

"As expected, no answer has miraculously appeared while writing this, but perhaps the writing has helped me understand the feelings that are controlling me. This does not seem a fitting way to end these writings, with the final answer being, *I don't know*. It seems there should be a happier ending, such as: *and they lived happily ever after*. But life, as we choose it, will go on. How *happily* will probably be more determined by *how I go from here* rather than *where I go*, so possibly the answer, *I don't know,* is not so bad.

"Rather than continue to ramble, hoping for answers to miraculously appear, I must conclude this writing. One last bit of wisdom or philosophy seems appropriate, though. I still believe everything in life seeks a balance, that nothing can ever be *good* without an equal amount of *bad*. If this is true, then a case can be made that nothing is *bad*, since what we call bad may be necessary for everything to remain in balance. Without rain, sunshine would not be appreciated; without pain, we cannot grow. If this is true, then I think I must be in the process of an amazing amount of growth. Sometimes I feel as if I have taken life's *best punch*, and if I am still standing, then nothing else can ever hurt me. I still believe that *nothing is either good or bad*; it is all in how we choose to see it. If things always strive to regain balance, then certainly this must be true. So I shall continue, trusting that some power greater than I will make all things right again.

"*Where do I go from here*? I still do not know the answer, but since I cannot continue to stand still, I must start down the road. Perhaps as I get farther along, I may better see where I am going. At least the adventure of the trip might prove exciting again.

"I will always love you, my dearest Lara, and you will always be a part of me. I will say *goodbye* for now."

Dad finally finishes his writing. I know that what he said about continuing with his life is true, and as always, I wish I could help him. Who knows? Perhaps I have. I am nearly certain that there were times during this writing when he felt my presence. Maybe he knows I was there, reading his words and sharing his feelings. Now that Dad has finished his writing, I feel the need to return and see if Mioki can provide any more answers for me.

Chapter Eight

My spiritual adviser, as I have begun to refer to Mioki, continues to help me try to understand this thing we call life. She has explained that we never really die, meaning that our soul continues to live forever. I feel the need to question her about all this, such as what is the meaning of death in the Biblical sense, and she explains that this refers simply to a transformation, much as how the new buds of spring replace the dead autumn leaves. I am still not a great student, but I am trying, and I hope Dad would be proud of me. Who knows, maybe I will even make the honor roll *here*. I do not mean to imply that we actually have classes, yet I know I am here to learn. Learning, I have discovered, is our primary purpose for being *there,* too. Being *here* is simply another part of life, but this is nearly impossible to understand while in the physical world.

I realize that Mioki cannot explain some things to me because I am not yet ready, and as she said, some things we must experience in order to understand. She says I am lucky to have an opportunity to spend so much time *there* with Dad, but that as time passes, I will feel less need to be there and then I will be drawn more strongly toward the light, or the ultimate love—the whole, or God. Mioki also says that I never seem to run out of questions, and I have even more now.

Mioki, there is something else I want to ask. Dad is still struggling with why my accident happened, and I also wonder why I was killed at age seventeen, when I had barely begun to get my life together. Can we ever know why these things happen? Like, why did my accident happen?

Yes, of course, Lara. Your accident happened because you were not paying attention to your driving.

What? Oh, I know that! But I mean why *did it happen?*

That is why, Lara.

But it—it cannot be that simple, can it? I mean, surely there must be some overall grand scheme for why these things happen. I thought maybe it was just time for me to leave there for some reason, or something like that. Will I ever know what that reason was?

You certainly ask lots of questions, Lara. I have told you that all these things will be made known to you soon enough. I will, however, answer this question. People often like to think some great force is watching over them, such as God or their guardian angel, which causes everything to happen for a reason. Sometimes this may be true, and this concept serves to help us explain the unexplainable. But Lara, you simply wrecked your car and killed your body because of actions you chose—free will, remember. If you need to know why something happens, just always remember cause and effect. Every action one takes, or even every thought one thinks, affects what happens to that individual, either then or sometime later in life. It also affects others. This does not mean that events occur for no reason or that there is no grand scheme; it simply means that we create or cause things to happen to us based on our actions—or reactions—which we, of course, can control.

So, you're saying then that I'm here simply because I wasn't looking at the road and lost control of my car? You mean that no higher force was acting to cause me to do that, just because it was my time to die?

That is correct, Lara, but do not assume this means the accident happened for no reason. Everything provides an opportunity for us to learn and grow. How else would we ever learn if we were not allowed to make mistakes? Remember when you were learning to walk? You were allowed to fall hundreds of times before you succeeded in walking. Life is much the same. We try, we fail, and from our mistakes or failures, we learn—assuming of course that when we fall, we get up and try again.

But Mioki, what about all this stuff about how God, or some mystical force, watches over us and controls everything that happens?

What about destiny, or predestination?

As I told you, Lara, you have free will in the physical state. What happens to you there is determined entirely by your past actions, decisions and thoughts, over which you alone exercise control. Do not try to make things seem more complicated than they are. You must understand, though, that we do sometimes ask for and receive help, such as in prayers; and as I said before, sometimes an angel appears to assist us through difficult times. Yet, even when we receive this kind of help, that too resulted from our own decisions and actions.

What about how Dad thinks this all happened as some sort of a punishment for him?

You do not really believe that is true, Lara, and neither does your father. He is simply trying to make sense of it all, but there is no way one can ever fully comprehend these things while in the physical state. We are not meant to understand everything while there, although some do comprehend more than others do. Your father is one of those. As I said, things happen to us as individuals based on our actions. From the results of our choices, we develop circumstances from which to learn. Since we are all connected as part of the whole, what happens to one affects others—all others, actually— but that may be too difficult for you to comprehend just yet. You can understand, though, that what happens to you affects your father, for example, just as what happens to him affects you. Your accident was not designed as a part of some grand scheme for your father's benefit, though. He will learn from this event, of course, and his past actions did have some effect on the accident's happening. One small change might have altered the outcome, you see—even some action from years before.

I will say that I understand, Mioki, but I'm not sure I really do. I know you are trying to keep things simple for me because I am so new to all this. I will think about what you have said, but I may have more questions later.

That will be all right, Lara. I will try to answer your questions if I can.

Okay, I just thought of one more, then. This

is sort of related, but not exactly. What about good and bad, or evil? I mean, bad things do happen to good people sometimes, right? And bad people have good things happen to them, too. Is there an evil force, or . . . well, you said everything comes from God, or is a part of God. What about bad or evil? Where does that come from?

You mean is there a Devil?

Uh, I guess so.

First, one must define the terms good *and* bad. *You must understand that everything is ultimately in karmic balance; that is, good and bad, day and night, light and dark, happy and sad, and so on. One extreme cannot exist without the other. Therefore, what you as an individual may perceive as bad could be a necessary part of the whole. And if so, is it really bad? Do you see what I mean?*

I, uh . . . I guess so.

You said that your father wrote something similar concerning this concept, so he must have a glimmer of how things are. Deep down, he must know that this did not happen as a punishment for him. From his and your perspective, your accident appears bad, but perhaps you can see now that it does not necessarily have to be bad. Does this make sense to you?

Sort of . . . but what about bad or evil people? Don't they exist? From what you say, I guess they must not, but are there not people who are worse? I mean, like murderers.

Lara, think about what I have told you and you can answer your own question. Remember the balance of extremes. If there is a God, then by definition, there must be a Devil, or some evil force, just as if there is good, then the concept of bad must also exist. So, if in the overall scheme, bad things must exist for there to be good, then are these things necessarily bad? Of course, certain actions are *wrong, meaning only that they produce undesirable results, or they do not please God. Sometimes we call these actions mistakes. But do they not all fit into the cause-and-effect relationship?*

I, uh, I guess so.

You see, Lara, when you as an individual make a mistake or take an inappropriate action, or do something **bad** *as you call it, then there are effects resulting from your action. Sometimes this affects you, sometimes others. In reality, your actions always affect you* **and** *all others. But back to your specific question. It is true that sometimes we do assume we perceive more bad traits in one person than in another. No person is either all bad or all good, however; we all have traits of both within. Remember, too, that what you perceive is not all that exists in what we call the heart or soul. We see actions and effects, but only God knows the extent or intent of what is inside. That is, only He knows the motivation for the actions one takes. And this motivation or intent is often more important than the action itself. This is why we are admonished not to judge our fellow man. This whole concept centers on the fact that some have had more learning experiences than others have, and consequently they know which actions produce positive and negative results. The more you learn, the more good you do, and the more good you do, the more you receive. But do not forget that in order to learn, you* *must be allowed to make mistakes. If we were perfect, we would no longer need to experience life as you know it. We would no longer be separated from the whole. If you are looking for a grand scheme, then I suppose you could say that is it.*

Wow! I guess I asked for that, didn't I? Will I ever be able to understand things the way you seem to understand them, Mioki?

Of course, you will, Lara. I have simply had more opportunities to make mistakes than you have. We are both still in an infancy stage, eternally speaking. We will learn together and as we are drawn toward the light, we will eventually become part of the whole again. Just remember that eventually *is almost immeasurable when dealing with eternity.*

Whatever you say, Mioki. But just one more question, okay?

All right, just one more this time. I must tell you again, do not try to absorb everything all at once. You have plenty of time to learn.

Okay, here goes. What about Heaven and Hell? Do they exist?

You already know the answer to that

question, Lara, but I will give you a simple answer: yes and no.

You always do that, Mioki*!* Explain, please*!*

All right, Lara, I am sorry. Do not take this all so seriously. Of course, you could answer the question yourself if you understood what I have just told you. Yes, Heaven and Hell exist, but they are not as most religions teach or as many people believe. This is much like the concept of good and evil; one cannot exist without the other. People primarily create their own hell, and it is not a place one goes as much as it is a condition created by refusal to accept the universal truths, failure to learn the lessons presented, and ultimately, it is simply a further separation from God. Every soul seeks to return to God, as God draws everyone toward Him, toward the light, toward the whole or the center. Some resist, however, and the more they resist, the worse their personal hell becomes. We cannot live apart from God, Lara, because we are a part of God, a portion of the whole, from which we cannot remain separated. When one tries to separate oneself from God, that is Hell. Now, do you think you can define Heaven?

Uh, I—I guess you would say it is when a person becomes whole, or one with God. Is that right, Mioki?

Yes, I am proud of you, Lara. I think you are beginning to make progress. Of course, this is still not so easy to understand; and therein lies the reason for our need to continue to gain experience. We need to be able to understand what it means to become one with God, or to return to the whole.

I feel that I have absorbed all I can from this session, or whatever I should call my experiences in this strange state. Anyway, I think something is going on *there,* so it is time to go back and see what has been happening while I have been away.

Chapter Nine

*T*oday I find some strange people in the house with Dad. I recognize the realtor lady, and realize these people are looking at the house, possibly to buy it. They have a daughter who looks about the same age I was when we moved here, so I encourage her into my old room, and then easily make her love it.

The girl can hardly contain herself. "Mom, Dad, look! My room already has a phone connection, and all these built-in shelves. Can we buy this house, pleeeease?"

Her father gives her a hard look. "We'll see, Andrea." Probably he does not want the realtor to see how anxious his daughter is. I can tell that the parents like the house, too, as they walk out onto the deck that runs across the back of the house and see the oak, maple and dogwood trees framing the back yard, with the boat dock and lake in the background. They think this looks like a scene from a picture postcard, and quickly they decide to submit an offer to buy the house.

As I watch them sign the contract, I think how much I will miss visiting Dad at our old house. I wish Dad had good memories of living here too, but I know he does not; so, I am glad that he is moving. He has decided to go back to California, and I think I might go with him. I wonder if he knows that I can be with him wherever he is. Occasionally, I feel that he senses my presence, but still he is uncertain, thinking it may be only in his mind.

Tonight is Dad's last night in the house. The movers are to arrive early tomorrow morning. Tracy was here this afternoon, but she and Dad have completed their good-byes and she has departed, leaving Dad alone tonight—or so he thinks. She begged him to go home with her, but Dad told her that he wants to spend his last night here, alone.

He has trouble going to sleep and lies awake for a long time, remembering all the things that happened here. In a way, he too is sad to be leaving, although he knows it is time. Sometime during the night, he gets up and walks into the room that was my bedroom. I feel his sorrow, his every emotion as he recalls the times he and I spent in this room together talking, sometimes until late into the night. None of those times was recent, of course. He reaches down and touches my bed, and then he sits on the edge.

After a few minutes, I begin to feel that Dad is trying to tell me something. Then suddenly a concept simply materializes in my mind, coming almost like a whispered prayer, as if I am receiving his thoughts, not with specific words but with feelings, much as my mentor, Mioki, communicates her messages to me.

Goodbye my Lara. I miss you and love you so much, and I will never forget you. Even the bad times were good.

Dad continues to sit on the edge of the bed and weep for several minutes.

After a while, he returns to bed, and when he drifts off to sleep in the early morning hours,

I somehow easily find my way into his dream—or what he *thinks* is a dream. Finally, I am able to tell him all the things I have wanted him to know so that he can go on with his life. I also ask him to forgive me, and I am certain he understands. I let him know that I understand how he feels, what he has been going through, and that I forgive him, if forgiveness is what he needs from me. I can feel his relief as he finally releases some of the pent-up guilt that has controlled him ever since the accident.

When Dad awakens the following morning, he does not consciously remember the dream, but I know the memory remains in his subconscious. Perhaps over time this will have a positive effect on him.

I ride with Dad as he drives across country, and as we travel, we both recall previous cross-country trips. I feel his sadness as he recognizes some particular town where we once stayed overnight during those trips. He even remembers a specific motel swimming pool where he and I frolicked in the water once after a long day's driving. I think I was nine years old then.

Suddenly I have an idea. I decide to see if I can make him stop at this same motel today. Unable to understand why, he does stop, although he had intended to drive for two more hours. After checking into the motel, he decides to put on his swimming trunks and go to the pool, so I meet him there and we swim together. I can almost feel the cool water, and I notice that my swimming has improved greatly. It takes hardly any effort at all now. After a few minutes, Dad gets out, sits on the edge of the pool and stares into the water for a while. Then he smiles as he remembers the last time we were here playing in the water, unwinding from a long day's driving. I smile, too, believing that he feels my presence now. And I am happy.

Finally, we are in California. I travel with Dad during the first few days as he visits many of the old places that hold such good memories for him, and for me, too. His first stop is at our previous house, the one with the swimming pool. He parks across the road from the house and just sits there in the car, recalling some of the good times we shared while living here. He notices the tall pine tree in the front yard, which was our first Christmas tree here, the only live tree we ever had. We planted it in the front yard the day after Christmas, and the tree is now nearly as tall as the two-story dwelling.

We each experience a combination of joy and sadness as we sit in front of the house, reliving many of the events that happened when we lived here. Dad remembers the time when I accidentally drained the swimming pool by turning the filter system to bypass in the wrong direction. He smiles now as he recalls how our yard flooded, sending water pouring into the street in front our house. He was so upset and embarrassed when our neighbors saw all that water. Next, he thinks of the time I helped him build a patio cover, how I played more than I worked. But he liked my being out there with him. Suddenly he sees a picture in his mind of me standing in the bottom of the swimming pool during its construction. That actual photograph is in the book of my life that he put together right after the accident.

Dad finally leaves and drives slowly through the neighborhood. Soon we arrive at the junior high school I attended, but Dad cannot stop; it makes him too sad. He then drives down a road heading into a canyon and immediately I recognize the area. This was once the trail where the rattlesnake incident occurred, although a four-lane, major road has been built through the canyon where the trail used to be. Dad and I picture the event as he pulls off the road and stops where he thinks we might have walked that day, although he cannot be certain. As he sits and thinks about that little girl who screamed *snake* so loudly, he both laughs and cries. He remembers killing the snake, and how I cried because I thought I had caused the poor creature to die. He then thinks again of how I grew to like reptiles, especially lizards, turtles and such, and how excited I was the weekend I brought home the pet turtle from school when I was in the fourth grade. I am surprised he can still remember the turtle's name. I had almost forgotten that the little pet turtle was called *Sprout*.

Soon we find ourselves in front of Sarah's house. She was my best friend here when we were in junior high school and Dad has not seen her since the accident. In a way, he wants to talk to her now, and almost goes to her door, but he cannot, and I understand his mixed feelings. He is afraid it might be embarrassing for her, and he does not know what he would say to her now, anyway. As he drives away, I think about how much I, too, would like to see Sarah now, but then I decide it might be better to remember her from before.

Dad does not drive around anymore today. He cannot handle any further emotional memories, I suppose, and I feel the same. He returns to the motel, intending to begin searching in earnest for a place to live commencing first thing tomorrow. I think he just today made the decision that he definitely wants to live here again, and I am glad.

Chapter Ten

One day a few weeks later, while Dad is unpacking and getting settled into the new house he purchased in San Diego—which coincidentally is only a few streets from where we lived before—he comes across a box. He immediately recognizes it as the box containing my notes, diaries and journals. He sits on the side of the bed for a few minutes, trying to decide whether to look at these things. I experience his mixed feelings. Although I am apprehensive about what he might find and how it might affect him, in a way I am glad he is considering reading these things.

After a while, Dad stands and slowly places the box on a shelf in the top of the closet. He then continues with his unpacking. A few minutes later, he feels drawn back into the bedroom where the box is stored. He takes it down from the closet shelf, places it on the bed and then sits for a long time, just staring at it. Finally, he takes out his knife and tentatively cuts the tape securing the top. Then he pulls back the flaps until he can see some of the notes and papers inside. I can feel his strong urge to read these things, yet at the same time, he is afraid of what he might find. And he feels that if he reads these notes, he might in some way be invading my privacy. This I understand, although I do not think it matters so much anymore. I find myself wishing with all my heart that he will find that note I wrote to him a few days before the accident, the one I never gave him.

    He begins taking some of the things out of the box and placing them on the bed. Then he starts sorting the items into categories. He finds three spiral notebooks containing journal entries, a small red diary with the key still in the lock, and several notes, perhaps hundreds of them. Most of these notes are folded into two-inch square packets, their corners tucked neatly inside themselves. Many have names written on the outside, and Dad is hesitant to read these. Some are from me to my friends, which either I never delivered, or they were returned and I kept them. He notices several notes from Lynn, and others addressed to her from me. I hope he does not read these.

Dad continues to sort through the notes, placing them in small piles on the bed. After a few minutes, he suddenly stops and picks up one of the notes. His hand begins to tremble as tears steal into his eyes. He has found the note with the word, *Dad*, printed on the outside and he is stunned, uncertain what he should do. For a long time, he continues to sit, just staring at the note, until I become afraid he is going to put it back with the others, and not even read it. I know he wonders why I wrote that note, but then never gave it to him.

Finally, he decides that I must have meant to give it to him, but perhaps was killed before I had a chance. Still, he considers for a long time whether to read it. In my mind, I scream: *Read it! Please, please read it, Dad. Go ahead, it's okay.*

His hands shake as he hesitantly begins unfolding the note, pulling out first one corner, then another. Again, I feel his uncertainty as he stops and looks intently at the piece of paper, which is still partially folded. Then he closes his eyes and I watch a tear fall onto the bed. Then another tear falls, this one landing on the note. He opens his eyes, blinks a few times, then rubs his eyes with the back of his hand and again stares at the note. I feel his heartache, and I understand his indecision about whether to read this note.

Read it, Dad! Please read it, I plead, softly.

Slowly, with trembling hands, he continues unfolding the single piece of crinkled paper. First, he notices the date at the top, December 8, 1989, and realizes this note was written only a few weeks before I was killed. His heartbeat quickens as he feels that this message is going to be significant, and again he hesitates, tears filling his eyes. I cannot help experiencing the crying feeling, too, as through his tears Dad finally allows his eyes to scan down to the contents of the note. I remember well the night I wrote it, and I try to remember why I never gave it to him, but this I cannot recall.

Dear Dad,

I really enjoyed that movie Chances Are last night. I wish we could do things like that more often - share things, I mean. I know it's my fault we don't, but last night was special, almost like old times, which I really miss. I just wanted to write this note telling you that I'm really sorry for everything. I know I've caused you a lot of gray hair and I feel real bad. I guess I dug my own hole, huh? Trust me, I'm as sick of trouble and lectures as much as you. I know it's kind of late, but believe me you will see some change! I know you've heard that a hundred times but this time you'll SEE a change. Just give me a chance (I guess that sounds familiar) I know I've said the same thing over and over. Maybe if you gave me some daily jobs or something, maybe I could start to learn some responsibility. Like a list when I get home from school with a few chores on it or something. Just a suggestion.

Well, I just wanted to remind you that I love you and I do have a lot of respect, even if I'm not the best at showing it. Maybe if you stopped always trying to have talks, we'd get some talking done. Well, I guess that's all I had to say. Except that I love you!

The note concludes with a drawing in the shape of a heart, with the word, *ME*, inside it.

Tears blur Dad's image of the heart, and he continues to weep for a long time. Slowly, things begin to become clear to him: his uncertainty about my problems; his regrets for never having resolved the issues between us; and his concerns about whether I would ever have come back. He knows now that I was trying to come back, and that in time I would have. He feels now that perhaps his Lara *has* come back. I wish I could tell him he is right.

Dad does not read any of the other notes or journals; somehow, they no longer matter. He folds the note and places it into his pocket, intending to find a special place for it later. Then slowly he replaces everything into the box and puts it back on the shelf. Someday soon he will burn these things, to never again be tempted to read my private writings. After all, he has already read the most significant, the one he was meant to read.

Chapter Eleven

Dad is nearly asleep when his miracle journey begins. Perhaps he is asleep and what follows is only a dream; yet, it feels so real. At first, he questions what is happening and why, as incredibly he finds himself again in that small country cemetery. He is walking down the dirt road that runs alongside the western edge. Gravel crunch beneath his feet and a warm breeze blows his hair into his eyes. Then the road turns and he finds himself walking beneath those tall maple trees growing just behind the cemetery.

A gentle breeze wafts across the grass and through the trees, conveying the sweet aroma of honeysuckle growing along the fencerows. He remembers that in his youth he used to suck the blossoms, and even now, he can almost taste the sweet elixir. It is springtime; flowers are blooming, birds are singing in the treetops and honeybees are buzzing around, collecting the plentiful nectar. The grass and trees are again coming alive with the greenness of a new beginning, and Dad's heart sings as he experiences a remarkable feeling of joy and love.

He stops and for a long time he just stands, staring up toward the treetops, watching as the leaves move gently in the wind. Memories of that last time he was here flood his consciousness and bring tears to his eyes. He remembers also the time he came here so many years ago, when he had to endure the other great loss of his life, the day my mother was buried. He has never been able to return to this place, except for that day when he had to leave me here, too.

After a while, he continues into the cemetery and approaches the headstones marking mine and my mother's graves. He kneels between the two, feeling the soft grass as his knees sink deeply into the plush cushion of Bermuda. His senses seem to intensify as he absorbs everything around him: the sweet aroma of the flowers and grass, the deep blue sky and gentle breeze. Somewhere in the distance he hears birds singing and the sound of music fills his heart, as tears flood his eyes.

Never has he felt closer to Lara than now, as he stares at the words printed across her small headstone:

LARA ALICIA MASTERSON
Born: November 10, 1972
Died: January 24, 1990.

He moves closer and touches the cold granite, his fingers caressing the letters. Wiping his eyes with the back of his hand, he again stares at the marker, allowing his fingers to move softly across the letters cut deeply into the stone. Closing his eyes now, he feels each letter of her name, his fingers moving one-by-one across the characters, L A R A, much as a blind person might read Braille. Time stands still as he kneels there, allowing his heart to become one with Lara's.

Some immeasurable time later, the tears cease to flow and he stands; something is drawing him toward those tall maple trees behind the graveyard. As he continues to walk in that direction, he hears the wind rustling softly through the leaves, and his eyes move upward toward the treetops swaying gently in the breeze. He remembers looking up at these same treetops the day Lara was buried. He had felt her presence then, and he senses her with him now, more strongly than he has yet felt since that day.

Suddenly the wind intensifies and he feels a familiar tickle as the breeze lifts the hair on the back of his neck and tugs at his shirt sleeve, the way he remembers Lara used to do as a little girl to get his attention. He hears birds singing in the treetops, one melody standing out among the others. Perhaps this is a mockingbird producing the tune that reminds him of *Lara's Theme* from the movie, *Doctor Zhivago.* Words from the song form in his memory: *Somewhere my love; there will be songs to sing . . .*

He stands there for a long time, filled with awe and wonder, his face squinted in a curious frown as he stares toward those treetops. He feels Lara's presence becoming even stronger, and somehow he knows now that she was here that other time, too—that perhaps she *was* in the wind in those treetops, just as he imagined.

Slowly the wind subsides, creating a soft rustling through the leaves and dancing lightly across the green grass. Closing his eyes, he senses Lara's presence even more strongly now. Then suddenly, from the direction of the treetops, a soft whisper drifts into his consciousness. He is not even surprised as he hears the words:

. . . the wind, Dad. I am the wind.

Too light to be held in his heart any longer, his pain suddenly lifts from him, rises into the air and is snatched away by the breeze.

Glancing back toward the tops of the tall maples, now swaying gently in the breeze, he utters a single word: *Lara*.

Then from the treetops, the whisper floats gently back to him: *I am the wind.*

Afterword

Eleven years have passed since we received that fateful phone call telling us the most horrible news a parent could ever imagine hearing. Sometimes now a whole day or two goes by when I do not think of her, or of the accident that took her life. Perhaps this simply means that I am finally able to function somewhat effectively again, although it can, of course, never be as it once was.

When a day or two passes and I do not think of her, invariably I will see her picture or some memory of long ago will flash into my mind, and all those feelings again come flooding into my consciousness. But the days—and particularly the nights—are a little easier now than they were during the first two or three years. No longer do I cringe every time the phone rings, as I did for such a long time—although sometimes I still find myself hesitating before picking up the receiver, particularly when a call comes in during the late evening or early morning.

As one final declaration, I must again reiterate that each of us has to find our own way to work through such tragedies as this—and what works for one may or may not work for another, for we are all products of our past environment. During times of extreme stress (and need I tell you that there is nothing more stressful than having to deal with the loss of a child), we almost always resort to whatever worked for us in the past when dealing with stressful situations.

There is no magic formula for getting through those lonely days and nights—no shortcuts. I have done it *my* way, just as each person must seek and find what works for them. No one can ever tell us how to get through this.

They say *time heals all things,* but in reality, the passage of time only makes dealing with the pain a little easier. It is a pain that will never go away, nor do we want the pain to stop, for it is a constant reminder that life is fleeting—so fragile that we should treat each precious moment we spend with our children (or any loved one) as if it might be the last. So tell them you love them, while you still can!

Additional copies can be ordered from:
Penman Publishing
P.O. Box 90087
Chattanooga, TN 37412
email: info@penmanpub.com
www.penmanpub.com
423-400-3292

Other Books by Rayford Hammond

THE ICE BREAKER INCIDENT
ISBN: 1-892614-20-0
Fiction: Adventure/Mystery
set on Navy Icebreaker in Antarctica,
New Zealand and Hawaii

RISING TO SEA LEVEL
ISBN: 0-9700486-2-9
Fiction: Inspirational account based on
author's loss of seventeen-year-old
daughter in automobile accident

THE SWALLOWS KNOW
ISBN: 1-892614-26-X
Fiction: Romance/Suspense set in
San Juan Capistrano, San Diego
and on Navy Cruiser in Long Beach, CA

Contact Penman Publishing to Order Copies.